Death at the C

Also By Susan Willis

The Curious Casefiles

Magazine Stories from the North East

Christmas Shambles in York

Clive's Christmas Crusades

The Christmas Tasters

The Guest for Christmas Lunch

The Man Who Loved Women

Dark Room Secrets

His Wife's Secret

The Bartlett Family Secrets

Northern Bake Off

You've Got Cake

A Business Affair

Is He Having an Affair

NO, CHEF, I Won't!

For all the friendly, good people of Whitley Bay. The welcome from Parkdean Resorts, where I spent a week in a caravan researching this novel. And, 'The Bound' bookstore who champion Northern authors.

Prologue

My knees begin to knock. Although I've written about dead bodies, I've never actually seen one. I swallow hard.

Her head is lolled back on the top step. She looks almost ethereal with a white puffed-up face. From what I remember she had a thin face, but now it seems twice the size.

Her eyes are half open as if she is looking down into the sea and her lips are blue. There are bits of seaweed tangled in her hair which has come out of the tight bun she'd had when I met her.

Chapter One

I don't mind admitting that at the age of thirty-one, I'm excited to be having my first holiday in a caravan. I am in the back of a taxi having left Whitley Bay metro station and travelling along the seafront towards the caravan park. The sun is shining, and the sea looks calm with gentle waves lapping onto the shore. It makes me smile.

The taxi turns into the caravan park and pulls up outside a low building with a reception sign and an arrow pointing to the side. I pull my big suitcase holding writing folders and probably more books than I need inside reception. I slot the strap of my laptop case onto my shoulder and gaze around at the posters on the walls of Whitley Bay and St. Mary's Lighthouse.

A shiver runs up my back. I'm not sure if it's because I write mystery and thriller stories, but I often have a second sense about strange happenings which are about to occur. And I am having one right now. Has something weird happened here in the past to make it feel eerie? Or, is something odd going to happen in the future? I shrug the feeling aside and look around the room.

It's a small square room with two doors to the left of the desk. There's a slight savoury soup smell but as it's just after one, I figure this lunchtime aroma makes sense. Usually, check-in is at four, but I've paid extra to arrive earlier which coincides with the train to Newcastle from York.

Behind a Perspex screen is a lady I guess to be in her sixties. She is looking down and typing quickly on a keyboard in front of her screen. I pull the strap of my laptop case further up my shoulder and try to wait patiently. This isn't easy. Bubbles of excitement are curling around my gut in eagerness to see the caravan which will be my home for the next two weeks.

There are leaflets on a stand in the corner about Seaton Delaval Hall, Tynemouth, and St. Mary's Lighthouse. I take a copy of each and a map of the caravan park. The glossy images on the leaflets look enticing and decide these will definitely be worth a visit. They'll be a great distraction in between long writing sessions when I need to stretch my legs.

The woman has greyish hair with a wide pink stripe at the front and is wearing a black suit with a name badge saying, Liz Mathews, Manager. I notice her long finger nails are the same bright pink as her hair. Whatever floats your boat, I think and can't help tapping my sandalled foot while I wait.

Eventually, she looks up and smiles. 'Hey,' she says pointing to my laptop case. 'You must be Clive Thompson?'

I recognise her voice from the telephone call when I made the booking and smile. 'Yep, that's me,' I say and look again at her badge. 'It's nice to meet you, Liz.'

I try to use people's names wherever possible because it's more friendly and I've found in the past that most individuals appreciate this. Obviously, Liz does because I watch her pull back her thin shoulders and preen a little.

'Well, I can't say we've ever had an author come to stay before,' she says patting the back of her hair.

Her face, which looks heavy with make-up, widens into a big smile and I can see the younger woman that she once was. She has big pale blue eyes which I'd call, baby-blue and can tell she must have been a real stunner.

I shrug my shoulders and smile. 'And, I've never had a caravan holiday either so that makes us quits.'

'Really?' she says and giggles while printing out a form. 'Not even when you were little?'

I shake my head and sign along the bottom of the form. For a split second my mind flies back to Doncaster where I was brought, or some would say, dragged up. A holiday was something I had never had in my childhood. With an alcoholic mother and drug dependant father all the benefit money had gone on their fixes. I'd never had so much as a trip to the seaside. My gran had taken me once to Conisbrough Castle for the day but that had been the month before she died when I was eleven.

I shake the old memories aside. 'Nope, not even then so I'm looking forward to these two weeks which should give me time to finish my novel,' I say. 'My fiancé, Barbara is working in Northern Island and our house in York always seems to be noisy with something happening to disturb me, so being off work, I fancied a change of scene.'

Liz smiles. Her face appears to have lost some of her fascination in yours truly, and I wonder if it was because I mentioned Barbara. Surely not, I think and begin to tap my foot again. Barbie, which is what I call my fiancé, often tells me that I am very naive when it comes to women and I'm an expert in misreading the signals - whatever that's supposed to mean.

Liz asks, 'Ahh, so what's the novel about? Is it set up here somewhere or in York where you live?'

I smile and run my hand through my hair. It still amazes me that readers love books that are written local to where they live. They seem to take great pleasure in reading about their town and the people. 'No,' I say. 'It's a crime thriller set in Durham City.'

She folds her arms across her chest and pretends to be affronted then cries aloud, 'Hey, what's Durham got that Whitley Bay hasn't?'

'Well,' I chuckle. 'They've got a cathedral and, a castle where my dead body might haunt the place.'

'Ooooh, that is creepy,' she says and visibly shivers.

We both laugh while she files away the form and gives me a ring with two keys.

'Well, I hope you enjoy your first caravan holiday,' she says. 'We see lots of people come here, turn off their mobile phones, let off steam, and have a relaxing time.'

I nod. 'That sounds right up my street.'

'So, the gate on the ramp up to the side door will be open,' she says. 'Then the door will have a cleaner's sticky label across it – just pull this firmly to break the seal and use the key.'

Pocketing the keys in my jeans, I thank her and turn to leave. Suddenly, a very old voice calls out, 'Lizzie!'

My eyes dart towards the room on the left of reception where the voice came from, and Liz gets up from her chair.

'Don't worry it's not a ghost,' she says and gives a throaty cackle. 'It's just my mam.'

She pushes open the door which had been left ajar. Now it is wide open I can see a very old lady sitting in a big armchair. She is rocking backwards and forwards with a knitted shawl around her shoulders.

Liz calls to her loudly, 'I'm coming, Mam, I've just been checking in another guest.'

I laugh and decide Liz's imitation cackle sounds as spooky as any witch could and shake my head. Twisting the handle of my suitcase to face me, I say, 'Thanks, Liz, I'll leave you to it and get going.'

She smiles and walks to the open door. 'Thanks, this is my mother, Audrey, who lives with me in our lodge on the park. She's ninety now and has Alzheimer's but today is a good day because at least she can remember my name. There are a few days when she doesn't know who I am or even who she is!'

Her words are said with humour, and I smile.

I raise my voice like Liz had done thinking the old lady may be deaf. 'It's nice to meet you, Mrs Mathews,' I call and then pull my case out of reception.

Once outside I take a deep breath of fresh sea air. I look at the colour coded map of the caravan park to get my bearings and follow the path down through the small car park to reach what is called the Entertainment Centre. According to the map, inside this building is an indoor swimming pool, a small supermarket, a café, and restaurant with an amusement slot-machine area for the children. I hear loud children's laughter and squealing then read the poster advertising a ventriloquist and face painting competition. They're having fun, I think and stride past the open doorway.

My heart soars as I walk past the outside of the swimming pool deciding an early morning swim will set me up every day before writing. I love to swim but must admit it's not something I do on a regular basis at home. Note to oneself, when I get home, I'll definitely start swimming again.

At school, I'd been disillusioned enough to think that if I achieved good reports then I would be worthy of my parents love and attention, but this hadn't happened. I'd been extraordinarily proud to get A+ in a geography project and, had been the first in my year to get a swimming certificate but none of my achievements had made any difference to them. However, the geography grade had helped me get the job in the travel agency so, as they say, I'll be grateful for small mercies.

I shrug at the awful memories and notice a small arrowed sign with the name, Ash Mews. My caravan should be number 24 and as I walk, I count up the numbers.

The caravans appear to be set out in rows of three with the last row facing the sea. I'm bubbling with excitement in the hope that I'll have a bit of a sea view. I walk in between two rows of caravans then spot number 24 which is indeed facing the sea. I hurry as much as possible dragging my case then hoot with delight.

Standing still I abandon my case on the grass then race around to the front of the van and almost cry with delight when I see the veranda. It has uninterrupted views straight across the sea to St. Mary's Lighthouse. Reached between the tides via a short causeway, St. Mary's has all the fascination of a miniature, part-time island, and I grin.

Oh, my days, I think and feel quite emotional. This is where I will sit to write every day for two whole weeks looking out to sea. I've got author friends on Facebook and Twitter that indulge themselves to writing retreats in exotic locations or in stately houses in the UK. They love to be secluded with their work so they can write uninterrupted by daily life.

I remember Barbie's favourite film, 'Love Actually' where Colin Firth plays an author and goes to Portugal on the coast to write. Of course, I've never been able to afford this, but hey I want to shout, who needs beaches in Thailand or Brazil when you can have just the same in good old Whitley Bay.

I laugh and retrieve my case longing to get inside the caravan to explore. I take out the key and think of Liz with her mother in reception.

Shaking my head, I walk along the ramp. Alzheimer's is such a dreadful and sometimes long drawn out disease. I know it's one of Barbie's fears because her mam is eighty-three now but thankfully, she is still bright and alert. I sigh, Liz must have a heart of gold to look after her mam here at the park.

Chapter Two

Liz Mathews

Liz sighed when Clive left reception and she headed in to see to her mam. She caught her own reflection in the mirror of what they called, their snug. With her deadly-high stiletto heels and swinging ear rings, Liz thought for sixty-two she was holding up quite well. She pulled up the waistband of her skinny jeans which still fitted nicely around her bottom and thin legs then grinned - just how it should be.

If she'd been twenty years younger, she'd have made a play for him because as well as being an author which sounded exciting to her, Clive was gorgeous looking. Polite and engaging in conversation he was tall, slim with blonde ruffled hair and those sparkling blue eyes were mesmerising. His fiancé was certainly a lucky woman, she thought kneeling down in front of her mam.

'I'm here, Mam,' she soothed. 'There's nothing to get worked up about. Everything's fine.'

Liz watched her settle back in the chair and stop rocking. She'd just started doing this in the last few months, but the doctor reassured her it was quite a normal reaction even on good days.

'Do you need the loo, Mam?' She asked stroking the top of her head. Mam liked this and on her bad days when she was very confused the stroking seemed to calm her down.

Audrey looked up towards the small window as though she was longing to escape. She never looked directly at Liz. Never had done, not even when she was a little girl. It was as if Mam couldn't bear to look into her eyes.

Liz felt her insides melt. Mam's small grey eyes appeared sunken in their sockets now and there wasn't an inch of her face which wasn't lined. Her hair had always been long and wound into a bun for as long as she could remember. Liz washed, dried, and combed the grey hair into the same shape every other day – she couldn't see the reason to change. In the past she'd offered to take her to the hairdressers and have it cut short, but Mam had scoffed and said, 'Now why would I want to do that?'

Audrey was a little rough and ready, as people say, and swore a bit but was kindness itself. Friends often told Liz she was her double.

Liz had never known her father, Duncan. Mam reckoned he did off when she was pregnant which in those days had been a great scandal. But Mam had held her head up, started the caravan site and raised her as good as any married mother would have done.

Mam used to say, 'There's someone for everyone out there.' So, aged thirty three, Liz had fallen in love and was engaged. However, her fiancé wanted to immigrate to Australia. Liz was desperate to go and although Audrey was on the ball back then, she just couldn't leave her. There'd only ever been the two of them.

Since then, Liz told other men she met that she'd missed her chance but tried not to sound bitter – she couldn't bear women who were sour and whined about past relationships.

Liz sighed, she couldn't feel resentful towards her mam because it had been her decision to stay. But she often wondered what an Australian lifestyle would have brought. She'd known back then that long distance relationships didn't last and had been proven right – he'd found someone else within six months. Mam hadn't said, I told you so, but instead she'd said, 'There'll be a better man around here for you somewhere.' And Liz had believed her. Even now she wasn't sure how she had actually ended up on her own.

Audrey had built up the site, they now called a caravan park, from five vans to what it was today around six hundred. The holiday season began from February 10th and continued right up to the New Year. They had a team of cleaners who worked hard and were paid a decent wage with pensions. The caravans were cleaned every week and bed linen changed alongside emptying rubbish bags. The park was 100% ownership where rates were paid to the park with half of the clients renting out their vans when not in use. They were all static caravans or bigger lodges.

Liz followed her mam's gaze through the window and along the small path to their big two bedroomed lodge in its own separate area.

In effect, it was like a bungalow with a little wood fence around the tended gardens. Mam had loved her plot and grew tomatoes in the small greenhouse at the back.

'Do you want to go home, Mam?' she asked. 'My shift is nearly finished so we could go and sit in the garden while the sun is out?'

Audrey nodded. She grabbed Liz by the hand and squeezed it firmly.

Liz smiled at her. 'Hey, it's okay, I'm not going anywhere,' she said knowing Mam didn't want to be on her own. Guests on the park might think it was cruel to have an old lady sitting in a room at her work place all day, but Audrey fretted more if she wasn't in her eyesight.

In years past, Mam had been very clever buying more land and expanding their business, which had made them a fair stash of money. So much so that Liz could sell up the business and retire now if she wanted. However, every time she'd gotten close to the decision, she backed off for one reason or another. Liz also knew it would be a huge change of lifestyle and worried if they moved from the park, it might make Audrey even more confused.

When she'd started forgetting things a few years ago Liz had alleviated her worst fear of going into a nursing home. 'That'll never happen, Mam,' she'd said. 'I'll keep you here with me for as long as I can.'

And she'd managed to keep that promise although there were days when it was uppermost

*in her mind and wondered if Audrey would
receive better care in a specialised unit or
hospital. Or could staff do an expert job of
caring for her? But their GP had said, 'Your
mam will never receive anything better than you
are doing, Liz.'*

*This had been a comfort because she really
wanted Mam to have the best. It's what she'd
always given her from the day she was born.*

*When first diagnosed with Alzheimer's she'd
done all the brain exercises with Audrey and
looked at old photographs hoping to keep her
memory intact. But it hadn't made any
difference – it was a cruel unforgiving disease.
She had watched her mam deteriorate over the
months until she was, as people say, a shadow of
her former self.*

*Physically, for a ninety year old lady she was
good. There was the occasional wet bed to
change, but Liz didn't mind this because they
had the huge laundry room where the cleaners
washed all the bed linen and towels from the
caravans. Audrey's appetite was healthy, she
was a little hard of hearing on occasions and
walked slower but had no physical disabilities.
The GP often said, 'In her body, Audrey is tip
top for her age – it's just her mental state which
is deteriorating.'*

*However, Liz wasn't a saint and there were
days when she felt like screaming at her mam.
The days when Audrey didn't know who she was
and what Liz did for her were trying, to say the*

least. This made her feel bad and not a nice person.

The dementia was exasperating. Some days Liz felt like running amok and smashing up everything in sight. This frustration of course wasn't vexing for Audrey because most of the time she was oblivious to what Liz saw as her hardship. There were occasions, especially at night if she didn't sleep well that she could quite easily throttle her mam.

Chapter Three

I lug my case inside and glance at the lounge seating area and open plan kitchen. Striding towards the veranda I throw open the doors. I'm directly facing the lighthouse in all its glory. The height of the white tower on the lighthouse seems to glisten in the sun. Next to it are two small low buildings. I'm not sure what these are, but figure when I cross over the causeway, I'll get more information.

I find two outdoor chairs and a small fold up table then immediately set them on the veranda facing the sea. Deciding to unpack later, I flop down into the chair and grin. The sky is blue with only two small clouds further out to sea. I take in deep breaths and exhale noisily loving the fresh sea air. As much as I love our city of York, we don't get this coastal air. I know if Barbie were here, she'd unpack straight away, but I just want to sit here, revel in my surroundings for a while and let my thoughts drift.

After a while I take a photograph of my view and WhatsApp it to Barbie with a funny message, 'Jealous, eh?'

I don't expect a reply as yet because I know she'll be working so I read the leaflets for Tynemouth, Seaton Delaval Hall, and the historic centre at St. Mary's. I'll need to know the high and low tidal times to fit in a visit to the lighthouse, I think and smile.

Inevitably, the novel I am writing comes to my mind which is always the case when I'm getting near to the end and unpack my laptop. I gulp at a bottle of orange juice and re-read the paragraph I'd corrected late last night.

My first novel was set in London because many crime stories are for some reason, and I'd done hour upon hour of research on Google. I had felt as if, to use an old saying, it was the blind leading the blind because I've never set foot in the capital. Following another author's advice, who is also a friend, I listened to his words of wisdom.

He'd said, 'I find it easier to write about a place if I know it well and the people who make up my characters. It's easier to imagine plots and scenes in my mind and you know what they say, Clive, fiction can be so much more interesting than real life itself.'

I had taken this on board and although I didn't want to use York because I work there, I did need to set it somewhere in the North East. When I'd started the novel and read out the plot to Barbie, she'd shouted, 'How about Durham? I know the city like the back of my hand!'

I'd hugged her and we'd spent a great weekend in Durham walking through the old streets, universities, and around Palace Green which is the area in front of the castle and cathedral. We had visited the Durham Miners Hall called, Redhill's and both of us had been fascinated at the artwork and statues of miners pulling coal trucks.

During those three days, I'd taken nearly two hundred photographs and felt as if I knew the city well. My novel takes place in the student accommodation, which if you have rich parents, is based in the actual castle itself. Of course, the castle has created an amazing atmospheric setting for a murder.

My main character is a newly promoted Detective Sergeant Jason Jennings. He's young, fit, and bang up to date. In fact, he makes me feel old even though he's a figure of my imagination. I smile thinking about him. Jason is someone I wish I could have been like in my younger days.

I correct a spelling mistake and re-read my paragraph aloud to see how it sounds.

The young blonde woman lay spreadeagled on the single bed. Jason bit his lip and bent over her. His breakfast muesli rose up and he swallowed hard. Jason could see before the forensics team arrived that she'd been mutilated and strangled because of the bruising around her thin neck. Blood dripped slowly from the end of the university-issue blanket. Two knives had been neatly placed on the end of the bed with the points facing the woman. Jason sighed at the senseless waste of such a beautiful girl and a young life.

My stomach groans with hunger now. I head into the bedroom and drop my suitcase on the floor then bounce on the bed like a child.

The double bedroom has a king-size bed and is en suite. Light oak panelling covers the walls with a turquoise head board. The linen is white and clean, and I know Barbie will love this. This oak panelling continues throughout the living area with large grey sofas which apparently fold down into two more beds. A big screen TV and small table in the corner lead into the open plan kitchen with all you'd need for a holiday. I grin knowing that I don't intend to do much cooking.

***

On a mission for food, I head out to explore the caravan park and sea front. I stride down the road from the park and turn right at the mini-roundabout. There's a wood bench facing the sea and I flop down to take in my surroundings. I lift my face up to the warm sunshine and inhale more of the fresh sea air. I've read how people think it's invigorating, and boy are they right. I'm filled with a sense of happiness and contentment.

To my left is a side road leading to the lighthouse car park and I see a few couples and dog walkers ambling down. The causeway must be open, I think but decide to leave this until another day when I can give it my full attention.

I look to my right along the coastline. The sand is golden, and many families are on the beach sunning themselves. Colourful windbreaks are stuck in the sand and people are sitting on fold-up chairs surrounded by bags. There are a few couples together lying stretched out on large beach towels applying sun lotion to their skins.

I stare at the gentle waves of the North Sea lapping up on the sand. I know from what Barbie has told me that the sea, even in the summer, will be cold. However, I smile at a few brave souls in the sea swimming while kids run in and out of the waves squealing.

Most of the children on the sand are laughing and running free on their school holidays. A couple of dads are with their children knee-deep in sand making sandcastles for them. I sigh knowing these children are the luckiest kids in the world. Not that they are learning how to build sand castles with a bucket and spade, but because their fathers are spending time with them. Which is something else I never had.

Although, I brighten, since then I've had a couple of cheap holidays in Spain with my ex-wife where we swam in the Mediterranean which was amazing. So, I figure, getting up to continue along the seafront, although I'd had a miserable childhood, I have certainly made the most of my later years.

I smell fish & chips in the air and grin. I'm tempted but shake my head. I don't want a big meal for lunch because it'll make me sluggish, and I'd rather have something light. Further along, I see a beachside café, called Art Links. It's a low building with a big cream signage along the top of exposed pink brick and huge arched windows. I decide it has been built into the original sand dunes. There are tables outside in the sun, but I wander inside and gasp.

The room inside has about ten small tables and chairs. There is a self-service counter laden with cakes, scones, salads and sandwiches. It's not the food which has stunned me, but the four walls which are covered in paintings and artworks.

I amble towards the far corner which is quieter and study some of the paintings - they are amazing. There are four black leather sofas and I perch on the end of an arm rest to gaze around at the artwork. Down the middle is a huge white divider frame with around sixty paintings hanging of local beauty spots by northern artists. Many are of St. Mary's lighthouse, of course, but Tynemouth Sands and Newcastle feature heavily alongside Holy Island.

I order and whilst I'm waiting, I decide to call into the caravan park shop on the way back to buy the necessities in life, toilet rolls, coffee, and milk. And maybe some non-necessities like a packet of Jammy Dodgers and Tunnock's chocolate wafers which are my favourites. Over the last few years, I've developed a sweet tooth and now struggle to drink coffee without dunking biscuits.

I hear Barbie's voice in my ear, 'A piece of fruit would be much better for you.' But I sigh, fruit doesn't eat right with hot coffee whereas biscuits work amazingly well. I justify with myself that I am on holiday so a few treats will go well with my happy relaxed mood. I wolf down the amazing chicken pesto and mozzarella ciabatta. Barbie would be proud of me, I think because she's always telling me off for eating what she calls junk food.

Afterwards, I continue looking at the other walls and study each painting in greater detail. One in particular of the lighthouse is painted with a view that is similar to what I look out at from my veranda. I wonder if the artist had stayed in caravan number 24? I smile appreciating the different colours of blues, pinks, and even purple which are beautiful in a stark contrast to the gleaming white lighthouse.

I decide to come back at the end of the holiday and buy the painting. Hopefully, Barbie will like it too because it is our home together now. I'd bought the house when I married my first wife, but she left me for an American basketball player and lives in Florida. However, Barbie has been living with me for eighteen months now and has transformed what seemed an empty shell of a house into our warm cosy home.

I continue further along the seafront past the crazy golf area and into the main part of Whitley Bay which is dominated by the huge white dome of what is known locally as The Spanish City. The whole of this area has been renovated with money from the National Lottery. There's a fitting tribute in the memorial gardens of a soldier statue in the centre surrounded by bedding plants. I nod in respect to see the Ukrainian flag on the post.

I read the words on the curved wall, Aaah, Whitley Bay. The Dome! The white Dome! It was the Taj Mahal to us.

I frown knowing Barbie usually calls it the Spanish City and wonder if people who live in Whitley Bay ever call it Taj Mahal? I'll need to ask her, I decide and stand in front of the dome looking up. It's huge with a row of flat buildings in front and a small turret type of tower all in white. On top of this tower and the dome are two white delicate statues which the information board tells me are, the dancing ladies who face each other.

I read about the renovation of the dome from an old funfair which had been declared unsafe and left to ruin. Apparently in 1910 when it was built a guy painted Spanish street scenes around the building, hence the older name.

There's more of a sea breeze now than earlier in the day. I stand on the beach watching big white foamy waves crash in three sequences getting smaller as they land on the sand. There's a few hardy northerners still seating on the sand with stripey windbreaks to protect them. I look back to where I've walked from and see the lighthouse in the distance standing tall and proud.

Along the promenade are four big circular shapes in copper and figure they're supposed to resemble sandcastles with flags sticking up and shell shapes cut in the sides. Hmm, I smile not being a lover of modern art. However, I'm impressed with these as the sun bounces off the gold and copper tones. It's only when I walk around to the front of them that I see benches inside where a family are eating their fish and chips. Clever use of the artwork, I think, although I can see the wind breezing through the shell shape because the woman's hair is in her face while she tries to eat.

I turn around to head back. Walking helps to clear my mind while I'm thinking through my plot and each of the chapters I've written and, how they lead into one another.

I take off my sandals and wade in the sea up to my ankles weaving in and out of the children who are splashing and laughing. Barbie is right, I think, the sea is cold but it's refreshing which makes my toes tingle.

I'm missing her already, however, she's due to fly into Newcastle airport on the last day of my holiday and we'll travel back to York together. Of course, we'll Zoom every night and talk on our mobiles, but I know that bed is going to be very empty without her small cuddly body.

Turning from the seafront, I return a different way through the opening to the caravan park and walk past a huge lodge which is separated from all of the others. It is set down a little gravel path with a picket fence around beautifully tended gardens. The small plaque on the fence says, Liz

and Audrey Mathews. I smile - it's good to see
they still live on the park.

Chapter Four

Audrey Mathews

Today was a good day for Audrey because at least she knew who she was and, more importantly where Lizzie was. Her name was Audrey Mathews and she owned and ran the caravan park. She repeated this sentence to herself over and over again desperate to keep her mind clear.

On her off days, which is what she called them when her mind felt fogged and clouded over, she couldn't grasp who she was and had no sense of reason. These were days when she felt a burden to others and thought it would be better if she didn't exist. It was frightening and as much as she tried, she couldn't seem to shift the fog from her mind. She relied upon seeing Lizzie moving around or the touch of her daughter's hand on her hair which was reassuring. It felt normal to her. It made her feel that she wasn't alone in the nightmare that had become her life.

Audrey never expected to live until this age after years of living the high life - drinking lager, smoking cigarettes and being overweight. She'd always thought she would have died of a heart attack or a stroke long before her ninetieth birthday. However, being confused with irrational thoughts and not knowing herself was something she hadn't foreseen.

On good days she had flashbacks to her younger days but knew she kept forgetting

*things. Important things. She knew her
daughter's face even when she was confused,
but often couldn't remember her name which
was so frustrating that she wanted to howl.*

*When they'd first uttered the word Alzheimer's
she'd been terrified. Audrey had mentioned to
the doctor how she was having problems
reading. All her life she'd read three- four books
a week. She had loved her trips along to the
library in Whitley Bay and could lose herself for
hours amongst the shelves full of books. It had
always been her escapism. However, the words
and sentences started to get jumbled up and
although she persevered, she struggled to get
through one book a week.*

*Also, in reception she would write messages in
the big diary for the cleaners and staff, but
everyone started to say they could not
understand what she wanted. They couldn't read
her writing and when she re-read the messages
neither could she. It was worse because her
memory of what the message had meant to say
had gone.*

*Audrey felt this was degrading because as her
sister, Maud often said, she'd always run a tight
ship. Their standards were high, and she had
been determined from the first week they opened
that all her guests would have a happy holiday
and be given good value for money which in
return would make them want to come back
again.*

Lizzie had joked and said, 'You write like a doctor on a prescription – no one can make head nor tail of it! I think we'll see the doctor to get you checked over.'

The doctor had tried to be kind by explaining the disease. 'Audrey,' he'd said. 'It's what we think of as a disappearing brain.'

Lizzie had pursed her lips in determination and said, 'Don't worry, Mam, we'll hit this head-on like everything else we've done!'

But Audrey had bitten the inside of her cheek while fear cursed through her body making her chest tighten. 'And that's fine, Lizzie,' she had said. 'But what happens when I don't know where my head is?'

She had cried in bed that night because she didn't want her brain to wither. She'd always been full of ideas which was how she had got the caravan park up and running. And the more ideas she thought of, the bigger it grew into the size it was today. Lizzie, of course had a greater input nowadays but up until a few years ago even she had come to her for advice.

Audrey had been married for three months to Liz's father, Duncan who turned out to be a cruel Scotsman with a mean streak running right through him. She'd met him during what they called, Scotch fortnight. This was when all factories used to close for two weeks holiday during the last week of July and first week of August. Hordes of Scottish people came down for their holidays to Whitley Bay, Tynemouth, and South Shields and their cash till rang out steadily. Duncan had been staying in one of her caravans with a group of his friends and from the first day he'd had a twinkle in his eye for her.

However, from the moment Lizzie was born she'd found it hard to look at her daughter's pale blue eyes because they were the same as Duncan's which sparkled when he was drunk and happy but looked vicious when he was sober.

She looked across to Lizzie now sitting on a chair opposite to her in the garden holding a glass of lemonade and asked, 'Which show is on tonight in the entertainment room?'

Lizzie tutted and clicked her tongue. 'Mam, we don't have shows nowadays.'

Audrey shook her head. 'Are you sure? I don't think it's a good idea to stop them because we always make good money. Have you booked Tom Jones in again? Or maybe get that young Engelbert Humperdinck because all the women love him!'

'Mam, as I've told you hundreds of times – this is not 1960! The days of the Bay City Rollers are long gone.'

She saw Lizzie wave at a man who passed by the garden fence. 'Cooee, Clive,' her daughter called out with that look in her eyes. She knew that type of look which got all women into trouble. The tall man waved back at us.

Was it Sebastian coming to get her? She felt her heart miss a beat with longing for it to be him. Although there were days when she struggled to remember things, the one and only thing that she knew with clarity was her love affair with Sebastian. She thought of how they'd made love on the lighthouse steps in the warm summer nights often in complete darkness but also on some nights lit up by the Northern Lights.

Audrey remembered his chocolate, dark brown eyes. He'd been, and still was on her lucid days, the love of her life. It's all she wanted to think about nowadays. She wasn't interested in the here and now, only Sebastian and how much she had loved him.

Chapter Five

I'm sitting out on the veranda in front of my laptop at seven in the morning with the sun on my face. The noise of what seemed like a hundred seagulls clattering and squalling along the roof of the caravan prevented my much longed-for lie in. Now they seemed to have disappeared for breakfast somewhere and I munch into a hot bacon sandwich with brown sauce.

I've decided Ashley Mews is the secluded end of the caravan park because the larger sections called, Dahlia Drive, Cedar Walk, and Millennium Gardens appear to be much noisier. Walking back from the café last night there seemed to be hundreds of kids racing around, parents shouting at them, and groups of tipsy hen parties and stag nights. Which I don't think makes for the quiet writing environment I need. So, yes, I decide this is the perfect spot.

Not that I've got anything against children but as I haven't had any of my own to manage and look after, I struggle with all that small children entail. Barbie is eighteen years older than I so we will never have our own family and I'm happy with this. She has a niece and nephew aged, eight and eleven who come to stay with us in York for weekends. And, although we have a fun time with them, I can't say I am sorry when they are picked up and taken home again.

I'm just starting to write my penultimate chapter when the side door of the next caravan on my right opens, and I can hear a couple arguing. Damn, I curse under my breath, I spoke too soon.

A middle-aged woman's voice shouts. 'But I'm not snooping! I'm just saying that I think he's somebody important.'

Then I hear an older man's husky voice chortle and say, 'You're getting like Hyacinth Bouquet.'

'No, I'm not!' She shouts back. 'And you'll be sorry when you realise, I'm right and he's a famous film actor or TV personality staying right next to us then you'll regret having the opportunity to speak to him.'

There's silence now. Are they talking about me? Surely not, I muse. I may be a lot of things, but an actor or presenter, I'm not. I hear a dog yelp and decide it sounds like a youngish puppy and then more ruffling noise.

The man's voice again sounds gruff and huffy now. 'Oh, there's no use talking to you sometimes, I'm taking Rusty for a walk.'

She shouts, 'Well, if you hang on a few minutes I'll come.'

Nah,' he grunts. 'We'd rather walk on our own, wouldn't we, Rusty.'

Out of the corner of my eye I see a man with a lively cockapoo puppy on a blue shiny lead and collar stomp out of the side door and slam it shut behind him.

Hmmm, I think, maybe Lord and Lady Grouch are to be avoided at all costs and smile. I've gotten into the habit now of giving people I meet nicknames. Which helps to create characters for my novels. I grin at the word, grouch. It says such a lot about the couple although I've never seen them yet – it fits their voices perfectly.

I keep my head down and start to write again but have lost my concentration and gaze over at the lighthouse. Perhaps a cool swim will help to get me back on track, I think, and rush inside, grab my trunks and a towel then head down to the pool.

***

It's a small pool but looks clean and well kept. I strip off in a changing room and plod down the steps into the shallow end amongst a few smaller children. I dip my shoulders underneath the cool blue water and sigh - it feels like bliss. I stride across to the opposite side away from the children.

The light smell of chlorine fills my nose and I'm transported back to the old pool in Doncaster and my lessons. I'd taken to swimming like a duck to water as the saying goes. The PE teacher had been surprised and delighted with my performance from an early stage. While others in my class had clung onto the side of the pool frightened to let go even with a floater pad, I'd been fearless.

When I think back now maybe it was because of the horrible violent atmosphere I lived in at home and a little thing like water held no trepidation for me. And, although I received very little attention or praise from my parents,

I'd thought the least I could do was to impress the teachers. My childish reasoning brings a lump to my throat now and I dip my head under the water. I notice two life guards sitting up in the high seats keeping a close eye on the children splashing in the shallow end and I begin with front crawl. After a few lengths I get into my stride.

I push the childhood recollections firmly out of my mind. I'm not sure why memories of Doncaster are making a comeback because it's something I rarely think about especially when I am with Barbie.

I'd had, as she often says, a troubled upbringing and at the age of fourteen had nicked stuff to buy booze. At first it had been for my alcoholic mother and then I got to like the effect when I drank it. The alcohol took me away from all the crap in the house, and it had also impressed my mates. I had got mixed up with a bad crowd although at the time I'd been pleased to be accepted into their gang. It was better than fending for myself and at least they wanted to spend time with me - which had been more than my parents did.

However, I'd ignored warning after warning from social workers until I had ended up in a young offenders' institution aged fifteen. I spent three years there and was released on my eighteenth birthday. One of the team leaders had called it a short sharp shock and it worked. It made me want to change my life and never be that horrible person again.

And, I muse I've done just that. Never again have I drunk more than a single glass of wine or beer, and although I wouldn't admit this to other men because it's not macho, I don't particularly like the taste anymore. And, I might add here that since then I've never taken a thing that didn't belong to me and wasn't mine.

When I first met Barbie, I hadn't told her about my past but when it all eventually came out, she'd forgiven my transgression and given us a second chance. Thank God, she believed in us, or shall I say, in me.

I push my arms out further with longer strokes and revel in slow continuous movements feeling all my muscles tense and relax in the correct order. This brings harmony and seems to restore my equilibrium.

Jeez, I think, I'd forgotten how much I enjoy this. Turning swiftly at each end I keep up the swift swimming strokes and stop counting after twelve lengths. I'm on a roll and loving every length and every minute. The muscles in my legs loosen and can feel that I am skimming through the water now oblivious to everything that is going on around me. I don't hear any noises not even when I turn my head to the side and gulp in deep breaths of air. My body is working automatically, and I let my mind go completely.

The train of thought I'd lost earlier on the veranda comes back to me and I write the paragraph in my mind knowing exactly what Jason Jennings is going to do to help the victim's family.

Jason stood next to the young girl's mother. He hadn't seen the dead girl since the day he'd found her in student accommodation. But he could remember the likeness and saw it now from mother to daughter. He could tell this mother was devastated to lose her girl. Jason could see the ravaged pain in her eyes at just the mention of her name. He saw her knees buckle just in time to catch her before she fell, found her a chair and a glass of water.

My arms are tiring and all of a sudden, I feel something catch my left foot. I lift my head and see two small girls laughing and throwing a beach ball to each other. The older, about ten years old laughs at me and throws the ball in my direction. I jump up to catch it and bat the ball back to her, but the smaller girl catches it and starts to splash me. I join in the laughter then hear a woman's voice call out.

'Hey, girls stop that - leave the man alone!'

I turn around to see a stunningly beautiful woman in a red bikini stride through the water towards me. The water is almost parting like the Red Sea did for Moses as her long toned legs advance. Not that I'm a devout Christian but I do remember the story from religious studies at school.

My mouth drops open. I figure she's around twenty-six or seven. With tight, wet, black curly hair, she reminds me of Halle Berry in the bikini coming out of the sea in the James Bond film. I can't help staring like a grinning idiot.

She reaches me and touches my shoulder gently. 'I'm so sorry that my girls have disturbed your swimming,' she says.

I glance down at her long, red painted fingernails and a musky perfume fills my nose. I nearly gasp out loud - she even smells good in the chlorine air. Her eyes are huge and what I describe in my novels as, hungry eyes, as if they're looking for their next conquest. Of which, I figure, she must have many.

The two girls stand next to her with heads bowed and both of them apologise.

'Hey, it's okay, I was finished my lengths anyway,' I say and both girls look up and giggle.

'All the same they shouldn't have done that,' she says and stretches out her hand. 'I'm Amber, and these two imps belong to me.'

I take her wet hand and notice my fingers look web-like with being in the water so long. I shake her hand firmly. 'Like I say, it's not a problem.'

I turn to climb up the steps and stupidly try to pull in my small, flabby gut. Barbie is right about eating junk food and I determine to get fit again.

'See you around,' she whispers.

I stride or wobble whichever way you want to look at it back into the changing room and take a sigh of relief.

I hurry back to my caravan for two reasons. First, to get far away from the suggestive tone in Amber's voice, and second, to write down my paragraph before I forget again.

Rattling away on the laptop, I've pulled on a sweater because the sea breeze is chilly, when I hear the same giggly laughter from the two girls in the pool. I glance to my left and see them and Amber stroll out onto the next veranda. Oh no, I think and my heart sinks, the gigglers are my neighbours on the other side to the grouches.

Chapter Six

Amber Brown

Amber showered herself and both girls then changed them all into clean shorts and T-Shirts. Hers just happened to be the shortest of denim shorts. Well, she thinks admiring her long legs and bottom in the full-length mirror, as her mum would say, 'If you've got it girl, then flaunt it!'

They'd arrived late last night from Middlesborough after waiting for a lift to Whitley Bay from a neighbour. The holiday was a gift from a school charity club because the girls had told teachers that they'd never been to the seaside. Amber had been mortified at first to think that everyone knew her business and poor financial state. Most months although she worked hard at two cleaning jobs - she counted every penny. Frustration often consumed her because at the age of twenty-seven she was no better off than she'd been as a young mother. She wanted so much more for her girls, and indeed for herself. But lately, her visits to the food bank were becoming more frequent, although Mum was a god-send and often kept them afloat.

She looked at her girls now tumbling from one twin bed to another and shrieking in laughter with bright shining eyes. She'd accepted the gift gratefully which was what Mum had told her to do. As well as the girls, it was the first time she'd stayed in a caravan and was impressed with the clean well-stocked rooms and facilities.

The caravan park itself was kitted-up for children with a great pool, and outside play area with slides, bouncy castle, and a trampoline. There were slot machines and musical rides which Amber knew would eat up her little bit of spending money so it would be best to give these a wide berth. Although her girls were very good and didn't hassle for material things like some kids did. They seemed to understand money was short which in itself was sad because like all mothers Amber wanted to give them the world on a plate. However, as long as the weather held, they'd be fine because they were only minutes away from the beach. If not, she had plans to take them to the cinema in Whitley Bay and mooch around the good charity shops.

Sipping a mug of coffee and flicking through the TV channels she thought of the guy in the pool and his sparkling blue eyes. He hadn't introduced himself though and had seemed to scarper away after she'd shaken his hand. It was fair to say that she had taken a liking to him and if it wasn't for her ex-boyfriend Kieran, hoping to join them later in the week she might have taken this a step further.

Her eldest daughter, Gabrielle, shouted, 'When is Dad coming?'

Amber's heart sank. She hated questions like this because most of the time she didn't have the answer. Kieran was a law unto himself. She'd been with him for ten years and they'd split up and got back together again more times than she could remember. He never contributed a penny to their upkeep and flitted in and out of their lives like a yo-yo. She hated him for doing this. Not so much for herself, although having her heart broken repeatedly was bad enough, but the hurt and anguish in her daughters' eyes was often more than she could bear.

The last time he'd disappeared, she had sworn would be the very last. Mum hated him with as much passion as she loved him, and Amber felt as if she was on a merry-go-round that she couldn't get off. He'd rang last week and more or less invited himself to the caravan stating it was his right to see the girls.

She called back to them now, 'It'll be later in the week because Dad is working so I'm not exactly sure what day he'll come.'

Amber hated lying to them. She knew there would come a day when neither of the girls would be pacified by her lies and they'd find out for themselves what a waste of space he really was. But, she sighed, he could be such a loveable waste of space. He often told her that she expected too much from him and that was why she felt disappointed. And, if she lowered her expectations, she wouldn't feel so bad. How's that for reverse psychology, Amber sighed.

Jayden, her youngest asked, 'Can we have pizza?'

Amber crawled up onto her knees and ran fingers through Jayden's curly black hair. She whispered in her ear, 'There's nothing I'd like more!'

Both girls ran outside onto the veranda and Amber saw them come to a halt then stare across over the white plastic railing to the next caravan. She got up and sauntered out. Amber gasped in surprise to see the man from the pool sitting on the next veranda typing furiously on a laptop.

She saw him look up and grinned. 'Hey, we're neighbours - how about that for a coincidence?'

Amber watched him smile and stand up. The girls ran to the railings and hung over them shouting out questions, 'What was he writing? Was it like school homework that they had to do? And where was his wife?'

She strolled over to him knowing he needed to be rescued. 'Girls,' she said. 'Leave the man alone - sorry, I don't know your name?'

'Oh, right,' he said. 'I'm Clive.'

She smiled and almost purred, 'We're here for a week's holiday, are you?'

He shook his head. 'No, actually, I'm here for two weeks to finish writing my book.'

She saw the same uneasiness in those eyes again when he quickly added, 'My finance, Barbara is joining me next week when she finishes work in Northern Ireland.'

Amber couldn't help but tease him now he'd used his fiancé as a safety net. The girls ran off

*back inside the caravan and she leaned right
over to him. Being tall and leggy, she knew he'd
be able to see her best asset in the denim shorts
and wiggled her bottom in the air.*

*'Hey, Clive,' she whispered. 'Wanna have a
little fun? Barbara need never know anything
about it.'*

*Amber grinned when she saw his jaw drop.
'And we're going to have pizza so, can I interest
you in a bottle of wine to go with it?'*

*She shrieked with laughter when Clive grabbed
his laptop and practically ran back inside his
caravan.*

*'Sorry,' he said. 'But Barbara is Zooming in a
few minutes, and I don't want to miss her.'*

*Amber heard him lock the veranda door,
shrugged her shoulders and sauntered back
inside.*

Chapter Seven

'No, Barbie,' I say looking at her little impish face on the laptop screen. 'I might have imagined the suggestive tone in the swimming pool from Amber, but I didn't imagine the come have some fun proposal.'

I can see her small grey eyes are teasing and she laughs. 'Well, you shouldn't be such a gorgeous hunk.'

I throw my head back and howl. God, I miss her. She makes me so happy. Since the day we met she has made me smile. Not that I'd felt abnormally unhappy before I bumped into her in The Shambles because I hadn't.

It had taken nearly two years and a few casual dates before I'd been able to say that I had put the breakup of my marriage well and truly behind me. But I had felt settled and content. Not deliriously happy, but who in these days could say they were? I know the last two years of a world-wide pandemic has had strange effects on most people and in a way, I'd felt good just to be able to come out of the other side never having the Corona Virus.

Barbie makes me cheerful whenever I look at her. If we are in a crowded room and I glance at her I feel myself melt inside with happiness. I often look at her and think, why me? How come I got so lucky? Because I know lots of men would give anything to have her. She's my life line and I can't wait to marry her in November.

I'll be her husband and so proud to have her as my wife.

'So,' I say and push my face closer to the screen. 'You're not jealous at all?'

Barbie comes closer to her computer now and I see she's had more highlights in her blonde hair. She runs her forefinger down the side of the screen as though she is stroking my face. 'Noooo, of course, I'm not. I can tell this woman, Amber has scared the pants off you,' she says. 'And if you had any intention of having some fun you wouldn't be telling me about it, would you?'

I sit back and nod. 'You've got my card marked alright – haven't you?'

She grins. 'Of course, I have, or I wouldn't be marrying you.'

Her eyes take on a soft look now and I know she's thinking about our wedding in the Bahamas. Even though she has a big family, as opposed to me only having a disabled grandfather in Scotland, it is second marriages for both of us. Therefore, we've decided to get married on a beach. Just the two of us but will have a reception when we get home in Durham.

I tell her all about Liz and Audrey Mathews, the grouchy argument from the caravan next door and my swim in the pool. 'So, I'm going to keep up swimming when we get home.'

Barbie giggles. 'Oh, you're going to be fit, toned, and suntanned for our wedding, are you?'

She has that gorgeous little smile on face, and I know it's because we are talking about the wedding. We aren't romantic in the sense of the word, and I do try to surprise her with little gestures, but we aren't soppy. My biggest gesture of course, was proposing to her on Christmas Eve when I got down on one knee in The Shambles. The fact that I slipped on the wet cobbles and Barbie caught me before I fell is beside the point, but it was a total surprise. My two female colleagues in the travel agency helped me secretly size an engagement ring and choose the stone which fortunately Barbie loved.

'Yeah,' I grin. 'I'll be turning heads on the beach alright.'

She tells me all about the contract and the people in her office. Barbie is a food technologist and a good one at that. I know this because being self-employed she is always in demand for her services.

I listen with interest about her day as she always has done with mine. We close our Zoom session kissing a finger and putting it on the screen. I feel settled now I have seen her and spend the rest of the night writing. It flows much easier, and I know I've written a great opening to my chapter. My character, Jason Jennings has solved the case and I'm cock-a-hoop.

**

The next morning with my laptop tucked under my arm and balancing my second cup of coffee, I head out onto the veranda. I sigh because the grouches are sitting out in the sun and Rusty runs over to railings to say hello. He strains to climb up at the white plastic railings and I cross over to the side and look at him. His golden brown hair falls around his eyes and big black nose then he tips his head onto one side and I melt inside. Although, I admit to not being a lover of all children, I do love animals and we have two cats at home. Spot and Stripe who are staying with a neighbour while I'm here.

'Morning,' Lady grouch says, and I reply with the same.

Lord grouch gets up and wanders over to the puppy ruffling his head. 'Sorry, if he disturbs your writing,' he says pointing to my laptop.

'Nah,' I say, 'He won't. I'm quite good at going into a zone and blanking out background noises - so don't worry.'

Lady grouch tips her sunglasses up onto her permed grey hair and smiles. 'I'm Celia Jarvis, and this is my husband, James.'

I figure there's a certain smugness in her voice when she says my husband. A little like the queen when she used to say, my husband and I. However, our poor queen can't say that now because both her and Prince Philip has passed.

I reckon they're in their late fifties maybe heading into their early sixties although it's hard to judge.

James is too far away to hold over his hand and shake, but he touches his brow in the old, touch-the-forelock gesture. I wonder if he's been in the services.

'It's Jim,' he says and glances back over his shoulder to his wife as though he's waiting for a derogatory comment.

However, she stares at me and asks, 'So, what are you writing - are you one of these people still working from home now?'

I see Jim shake his head slightly and tut at her direct questioning, but I smile at them, so they know I don't mind.

'No, I'm Clive,' I say. 'Clive Thompson but I don't work from home. I'm an author and am trying to finish my second novel.'

I can see Jim pull his shoulders back and look visibly impressed although I don't know why. Celia advances towards Jim and Rusty nudging the puppy out of the way with her knee so she can get as close to the railings as possible. Rusty rubs himself against Jim's leg who automatically ruffles his head again.

Celia simpers, 'Oh, wow! You see, Jim we are living next door to a famous author – I just knew it.'

I shuffle my sandals and look down at the white boarding. 'Em, well, I'm not famous at all,' I say. 'I don't even have a publisher at the moment, but my first novel is on Amazon.'

'Well, Clive,' she says. 'If you're on your own you must come to us for tea and tell Jim all about your novel – he loves reading especially crime thrillers.'

I sigh. It's the last thing I want to do but know if I refuse it'll seem bad-mannered. And, although I usually pride myself in being a quick-thinker, I can't think of a single excuse, and mumble, 'Okay, thanks.'

'About four?' Celia trills in an OTT voice and I nod.

She hurries inside their caravan in a flurry and Jim pulls Rusty by the collar away from the railings. 'We'll let you get on writing then,' he says and smiles.

I tap on their caravan side door just before four in the afternoon. Jim opens the door and Rusty practically throws himself at me. I stroke his long floppy ears and he stops yapping then rolls on the carpet next to me loving my petting.

'Come in, Clive,' Jim says and eases Rusty aside carefully with his foot. Their caravan is more like one of the upgrade lodges that I was offered when I rang to book but on my own, and at £600 a week I declined.

Celia is fussing around with tea plates and teapot talking all the while. I look at the row of nick-nacks on the ledge above the electric fire and the photographs in frames covering the walls. Working in a travel agency, I can see they are well known tourist attractions in Devon, Cornwall, and the Scottish Highlands. I comment upon this, and Jim tells me about each place, and how they used to tour in their own caravan.

Touring is something I've never thought about before and wonder if Barbie would like being on the move for holidays in different areas. But there again because she travels for work, she would probably prefer to stay in one place.

Jim says, 'However, now we are in this static caravan every weekend and spend most of the summer here too.'

Jim looks disgruntled about this and while Celia talks about the park and its facilities. I get the distinct impression that Jim would rather still be on the move.

'Now,' Celia says carrying the teapot to the table. 'Come and sit down here.'

She waves me over to slide into the corner unit around the square table which is laden with food. Neatly trimmed prawn sandwiches, small sausage rolls, raspberry butterfly cakes, and cream horns are on white china plates. I can't help licking my lips and visualise telling Barbie on text later about the spread of food.

Celia shuffles onto the seat next to me and Jim sits opposite with Rusty by his feet.

'I had Jim pick us these big, fresh prawns from North Shields quay and they're from today's catch so they should be good,' she says pouring tea into matching china cups.

I pray that I don't smash or spill anything onto the pristine white table cloth. Honestly, I'd thought that caravan holidays were about making do with plastic picnic utensils - obviously, not so for Celia.

'And,' she brags waving her hand around in the air. 'As you can see, we are all top notch here compared to the older more run-down caravans. We've a slow cooker which comes in handy, a top of the range microwave, dishwasher, and this forty inch TV set.'

I pick up a prawn sandwich and nod. 'Yeah, that's certainly a big screen,' I say.

It looks hideously out of place in the small room. The TV should be in a huge drawing room in a stately home somewhere and I smile thinking that Celia should be there too.

Jim looks to be the strong silent type who permanently raises his eyebrows behind her back when she is boasting. I try to imagine them both together when they were younger and in love.

There's a photograph in a gold frame on one of the ledges and Celia looks beautiful in a long, white wedding dress. Barbie has said that she's not going to have a traditional wedding dress when we get hitched because she had all of the customary hype when she first married in her twenties. However, I do wonder if she is playing our wedding down because of my feelings. I'd stressed from the beginning that I would like it to be low-key. Now, I sigh because as the saying goes, I do want her to have everything her heart desires. I want Barbie to have the happiest day ever.

I can see that Celia had everything that she desired on her wedding day because there's a hint of smug satisfaction playing around her lips on the photograph. I stare at her twisted thin lips now which are painted with bright red lipstick as she sips her tea. The lipstick leaves a red mark on the tea cup.

She pouts. 'You know, it was always a better class of people around here when we first came,' she says. 'But the owners now have gone right downhill - there's some real riff raff hanging around!'

I remember the argument I'd heard yesterday and agree with Jim's accusation that she was like Hyacinth Bouquet with her tea parties and can't help wondering if she held candlelight suppers too. However, I decide that she reminds me more of the Les Dawson sketches where two older ladies, Cissie and Ada play housewives with their arms folded under huge bosoms.

Celia is as fat as Jim is thin. She's wearing brown thick-soled loafers which I think means she is steady footed. A cream skirt, pink silk blouse and matching cardigan. This is maybe her 'friends for tea' outfit, I think and smile. They definitely look like what Barbie calls, the gin and tonic brigade.

The fresh taste of salty-sea prawns makes my mouth tingle. 'Oh, wow,' I say. 'These prawns are amazing - they're really plump and so juicy.'

'Yes, they're good,' Celia mutters in between chewing her sandwich. 'You did a great job, James getting these prawns.'

I suppose any other man would look pleased at the compliment but Jim only half smiles. It's as though he's heard all this before and it's back-handed praise. I glance at the pile of wool and crochet blanket by side of settee and imagine Celia being industrious of an evening and Jim ignoring her with his head stuck in a book.

I reach for a sausage roll which is warm and savoury, and I munch through it happily. Whatever I think of Celia, I can't fault the food she has laid out. 'This tea is great, Celia,' I say. 'Without knowing I think you've picked all of my favourites here.'

She simpers and pats the back of her permed hair. 'Well, come on, Clive, take a few more sausage rolls – there's more than enough.'

Jim chomps through another prawn sandwich and begins to tell me about the books he likes to read. Chatting together, I realise we have a common love of Ian Rankin and his Rebus novels.

'And,' Jim says. 'Have you read Val McDermid's book?'

I shake my head and stuff another bite of sausage roll into my mouth. 'No, not yet.'

Jim grins. 'Well, Val just lives a little further up the coast and her book is called simply, 1979.'

'Does she?' I ask and nod. 'I'll have to look out for that one but at the moment I'm concentrating upon getting mine finished then I can relax and catch up on my TBR pile.'

Celia raises a pencilled eyebrow. 'And, what does that mean?'

I try to swallow down the sausage roll but Jim answers for me, 'It means, he has a list of books, To Be Read.'

Jim asks about my novel on Amazon and never wanting to miss the chance of a sale I tell him all about it and pull a business card from my jean pocket. 'You'll find it under my name and if you do read it, I hope you enjoy the story.'

Refusing more tea and a drink with the excuse that Barbie is ringing shortly, I tell Celia about my fiancé then head back to the quiet of my own caravan.

Chapter Eight

I head out the next morning but when I reach the reception area, I see two police cars outside and sigh wondering if there has been trouble for Liz on the park. I remember the shivery feeling I'd had on the first day in reception and nod in satisfaction at my gut instinct. Maybe it was proving me right again and something was about to happen?

A few theories pass through my mind - burglaries or unpaid accounts or damage from drunken parties? I think of my belongings in the caravan and hope it's not the former. Not that I have anything of great cost but it's more sentimental value. My laptop isn't a new model in fact compared to others it's old and battered, I suppose. But it's mine and the space bar is shiny on the end because of the way I type. And I love it.

I continue down to the Entertainment Centre and hear the girls arguing in the kids' area which has musical rides and slot machines. They're not giggling today. I sigh and hear Amber shouting at them. I feel sorry for her especially on a day like today when it's damp weather. She's probably been stuck in the caravan alone trying to entertain the girls.

As far as I can tell, most of the children's entertainment is arranged for outside in good weather like cricket, tennis, and football competitions. They're usually held in the big field area with family teams, however on a wet day there's not much to keep them occupied other than the amusements and slot machines. I grin knowing for adults there's always the highlights of Bingo of an evening in the bar area.

I see Amber standing with her back to one of the slot machines looking frazzled. She's dressed in tracksuit bottoms and a black shirt. Her beautiful jaw looks clenched, and I watch her run a hand through her hair. This is unusual because I've noticed over the last few days that Amber is vivacious, fun-loving, and very sociable. She seems to have a kind word and a smile for everyone on the park. But not today.

Not wanting to get involved or into another awkward moment with the leggy beauty, I simply wave and set off on a long walk.

***

Feeling refreshed, I head back to the veranda to write. On the way up the gravel path, I turn at the call of my name.

'Hey there, James,' I say waiting on the path for him to catch up.

'Er, it's Jim,' he says and furrows his eyebrows. 'Celia is the only person who calls me James and I hate it.'

I take note and mutter a soft apology. Rusty races up to me and I bend down and stroke his long ears. His hair is cut in short straight lengths around his face which look full of mischief. Again, my heart melts.

In a grey shirt and slacks, Jim looks stick thin.
He's at least six foot two if not more because
I've noticed how he dips his head to go inside
the caravan. He's puffing on a vape as though
his life depends upon it. Jim is what I would call
dour looking until he smiles then his face takes
on a more pleasant appearance. Although his
smile often looks stretched as though it's costing
him money to make the gesture.

I fall into step beside him. 'Hey, I was
wondering what's going on? There's been two
police cars outside reception since this morning
and they're still there now.'

Jim nods and I can tell he knows something.
'Ah, well, apparently, Audrey is missing. She
hasn't been seen this morning and Liz is worried
sick,' he says. 'Liz took her breakfast into the
bedroom as usual, and she wasn't there.'

My heart sinks thinking of the vulnerable old
lady. 'Oh, no, and has she been out all night?'

Jim shrugs. 'Apparently the gossips are saying
that she had been in her bedroom at ten last
night when Liz took her cocoa.'

I keep pace with Jim's brisk walk and nod.
'Ah, right.'

Jim chortles. 'I bet that detective mind of yours
is working overtime trying to think of what's
happened and where she is?'

I smile and decide he's right. My mind is in a
whirl and wonder if I should call to see Liz and
offer my help. Not that there's much I could do

but give support. 'Poor Liz must be demented with worry.'

Jim sighs. 'It's the bloody old woman who's demented and deranged,' he says.

I stop and look at him because he's used such a brusque tone in his voice and manner – there's not a smattering of sympathy for Audrey.

We've reached the back of my caravan and Jim leans against the boarding. 'Celia keeps telling everyone that she thinks I've got early onset Alzheimer's because I'm always forgetting things, but I'm not!' He almost shouts. 'It's simply that I turn a blind eye or deaf ear to her bloody ranting.'

I'm not sure how to respond to this and wonder how Barbie would tackle the conversation. She's good at talking to people in a caring manner that I often lack. So, I settle for, 'And have you noticed that you're forgetting things?'

'Maybe sometimes,' he mutters quietly and looks down kicking at a few pebbles on the path. 'But only minor things – I don't forget the big things in life.'

'Well,' I say. 'Perhaps a visit to the doctor might help because if it's not Alzheimer's then you'll be relieved – won't you?'

His slight shoulders droop and he has a haunted look in his eyes as though he's forgotten I'm here and he's not alone. 'I hate being anywhere near Audrey,' he mutters through clenched teeth. 'It really bothers me in case I end up like her – as mad as a box of frogs!'

I can't believe he's just said this in such an uncaring manner. 'Jeez, that's going a bit far – isn't it, Jim?'

I see his eyes wash with tears then realise how upset he is and how dog-weary he looks. His cheeks flush and his chin quivers. I pray he isn't going to cry. I'm not good at emotional outbursts and wonder if I should fetch Celia. Although this might not be a good idea because Celia seems to be an outlet for his irritation, and it might make him worse.

Wringing his hands together, Jim continues, 'Well, I'd rather be dead than live like her in a continual deranged state – have you seen how her eyes are glazed over and blank? You can tell her brain is dead, well at least, I can,' he snorts. 'And that supercilious smile she has on her face. Ha! It's as though she's living the bloody dream – it's ridiculous – a meaningless existence.'

I shake my head. 'But Liz told me she does have some lucid days and if she looks happy and content then she can't be suffering – can she?'

Jim shrugs, 'All I know is that ending up like that is my biggest dread - can you imagine being trapped in a room with Celia all day?'

I can't and shudder slightly. I see real fear in his eyes and watch his face wince in distain when he says, 'If Audrey was an animal, like a horse – she'd be put to sleep with an end to her bloody torment!'

I can understand his frustration. Is this a rational response to the thought that he might have Alzheimer's disease? It's obviously an overreaction and I sigh at his oppressive outlook. However, I'm not in his situation so shouldn't make assumptions to his state of mind.

Although, I've just met Liz and Audrey, I realise Jim and Celia will have known them for years, so I ask about them.

Jim nods. 'Well, Liz is as rough as a badger and Celia reckons her language can turn the air blue,' he says and chortles. 'But she's very kind and obliging. And years ago, when they had the big shows in the Entertainment Centre, she had a reputation for being a bit of a go-er, if you know what I mean?'

He nudges me and I smile. Jim holds up his hands and slopes off to the side door of his caravan where Rusty is waiting patiently on the steps for him.

Chapter Nine

Celia Jarvis

*Celia is worried about her husband, Jim who
has been behaving very strangely of late. In fact,
she thinks he's been steadily getting worse over
the last three months. He gets up through the
night with bad dreams that seem so traumatic,
they're more like nightmares. During these
episodes, he shouts and rambles incoherent
words which she can't understand then paces
about the caravan from room to room. Often, he
wakes Rusty who scampers about behind him not
knowing what's happening and then runs into
their bedroom to jump up on the bed quivering.*

*She's mentioned a few times to Jim how he
doesn't seem to be taking in details and
forgetting conversations they've just had.
Yesterday, she'd said. 'I've said that to you
three times already this morning!'*

*'Yeah, well, you go on so much about things,'
he'd shouted. 'I just switch off!'*

*He'd huffed and stormed out with Rusty. Celia
knew she was what people called a fuss pot and
sighed. Other women had children and
grandchildren to worry over whereas she
hadn't. Therefore, she fretted over material
things. Where another woman would be proud of
her son's achievements, she glowed over her
new Dyson hoover. Sad but true.*

*However, Celia knew Jim as well as she knew
herself and could tell he had problems. In the*

*past he'd been razor-sharp at picking things up,
but now it was as if he couldn't organise his
thoughts into a proper answer? And, she
couldn't keep his attention for long either before
he changed the subject.*

*Celia picked up a duster and swiped it over an
already spotlessly clean counter top. She
remembered his face this morning when he'd
first woken. After forty years of marriage Celia
was so used to seeing the same man every day
that she'd stopped looking at him properly. But
she did this morning. She had propped herself
up on her elbow and stared at his face. He
wasn't eating full meals and losing weight
therefore his face was thin, and some would
even say, gaunt.*

*It was the face she'd fallen for when they met.
And the same pleasant smiling expression he'd
worn on their wedding day. He had looked, as
her mother said, 'Like the cat who'd got the
cream.'*

*But now, Celia sighed, he looked dreadful.
Troubled and maybe even haunted by something
– but what? They had no problems as far as she
could tell – they were rubbing along together
like they'd always done. They loved their
caravan and had many great memories of
touring and a good circle of friends who Jim
liked.*

*After their first ten years of marriage trying to
have children they'd long since come to terms
with the fact that it was never going to happen.*

Specialists had done their tests which proved there was no reason why she couldn't fall pregnant. It just hadn't happened.

There were no money problems because both had retired with good pensions and she'd always been, if not prudent, then careful with housekeeping. Jim had been an accountant for a local firm but was glad to finish work or at least that's what he always told people.

He'd often said, 'It's nice not to have my head full of figures and numbers every day and I can read to my heart's content.'

Which is what he does, she thought running a hand over her forehead in frustration. So, what was it? Was it her? Could he have met someone else? But she shook her head and scoffed at this notion. Jim was so naïve and shy he wouldn't know what to do with another woman. Upon this she was certain.

Which posed the question – was there something seriously wrong and he wasn't telling her? A stomach complaint, his heart, or the dreaded word, cancer. She'd tried on a few occasions to get him to make a doctor's appointment, but he had refused point-blank stating, 'There's nothing wrong with me!'

Celia switched on the kettle and spooned coffee into her mug. The only thing he seemed to talk about at the moment was how Audrey was missing and how distraught poor Liz must be, which Celia supposed was like everyone else.

Chapter Ten

I hurry inside the caravan, check that everything is as it should be and then sigh with relief. The conversation I've just had with Jim is worrying to say the least and I chew my bottom lip thinking of his words, mad as a box of frogs.

Maybe he knows something about Audrey's disappearance? Nah, I shake my head knowing I am jumping to conclusions. Jim is right and I'm letting my inquisitive mind run away with me.

I open my laptop but sit staring at the screen in total blankness. The caravan is silent other than the fridge humming away to itself. I look around at the sofas and cushions which are in disarray from where I'd watched TV last night. I can see the shape from my head in the big, soft cushion and think of Barbie and me back at home snuggled in our squashy settee together.

I swallow a lump in my throat. I seem to be missing her more here on holiday than I do when I am at home. Although, I reason that's probably because I'm at work and my mind is more focused. I tut, knowing my mind should be totally focused on my novel which is the reason I came here – to write.

Words and sentences which usually flow freely don't come. I can't seem to switch off from the fact that Audrey is missing. I grab my jacket once more and decided to go and see Liz. She'll probably have friends and family around her, but I can at least offer some support. There may be something practical I can lend a hand with.

***

A young blonde policewoman is standing in reception when I open the main doors. I haven't been back inside since the morning I checked-in and decide that it feels much longer than three days ago.

I explain who I am and enquire after Liz.

The policewoman turns her back and pops her head around the door behind the reception desk. It's the same snug room that I'd seen Audrey sitting in the first day I arrived. I notice the police woman's long hair that is twirled up under her flat black cap and wonder if she is hot in the chunky, yellow high-vis jacket.

The police woman ushers me behind the screen and desk.

'You can see her now,' she says, and I enter the room.

I gasp in shock at the sight of Liz. She looks like she's aged ten years since I waved to her in their garden on Saturday when she'd looked summery in flowery leg-ins and a red blouse. Now she is wearing an old denim shirt and scruffy jogger bottoms. The pink stripe in her hair is hardly noticeable because her grey locks are lank and hanging over her face. She's sitting in the big chair where Audrey had sat and is hugging a furry white cushion to her chest as though it was a baby.

Liz looks up at me and whispers, 'Oh, Clive, where is she? They've rang around all the hospitals in the area and no one with her description has been admitted.'

I sit down in the chair opposite and take one of her hands in mine. I smell smoke hanging in the room and notice the ashtray on the coffee table with cigarette buts.

I only tried a cigarette once when I was twelve and coughed my insides out so decided it wasn't for me. And Barbie hates the smell, but I can't say I do – I'm not one of the anti-smoking campaigners. I'm more of a live and let live type of guy, and if people, like Liz, find comfort in a cigarette during a stressful time then so be it. Although I am aware of the dangerous health effects of smoking tobacco, I reckon it must be difficult nowadays for heavy smokers because there's not many places where they can legally light-up.

Liz sobs and although I don't want to gasp again when I see her baby-blue eyes full of tears and without make-up she looks more like Audrey's age than her own. I swallow down the shock and try my hardest to smile encouragingly.

I think back to the paragraph I'd written for my book about Jason Jennings comforting a dead girl's mother in Durham and know I've used the correct word, ravaged. Liz looks completely ravaged by grief and involuntarily I shudder.

'I'm so sorry this has happened, Liz,' I say and squeeze her hand. 'But I'm sure they'll find her.'

She nods. 'I've been telling myself that since early this morning but the more hours that tick by the less likely I think that'll happen!'

She looks up at the clock on the wall and in the silence of the room I hear the loud tick.

As though she has read my mind, Liz, says, 'Mam likes that clock because even if she can't see the hands or reason what time of day it is she knows it's a clock on the wall.'

I look around the empty room and wonder why Liz is on her own. 'Have you no friends or family that could be with you?'

Liz shakes her head. 'No, we've an aunt and cousin down in Devon but there's only ever been me and Mam.'

At this, she starts to sob and reaches forward to take a tissue out of the box on the coffee table. I notice a full mug of coffee that is cold which she obviously hasn't drank. There's a water cooler in the corner and I ask, 'Can I get you a cold drink – water?'

She shakes her head. 'No, thanks, I can't seem to swallow anything.'

I'm not sure if Liz wants me here and whether to talk or remain silent. I reckon it's best to ask, 'Well, I just popped in to see how you are and what was happening, but I can go if you want to be on your own?'

I ease up from the chair.

Liz grabs my hand. 'No, stay,' she says. 'It's nice not to be alone with my thoughts.'

I nod and slink back into the chair. 'Okay, so do you think Audrey has been out all night?'

Liz wipes the paper tissue over her wet face. 'I don't know!' She wails. 'We just did the usual. The doctor told me years ago when she first began to get confused to try and keep daily activities in a routine. So, we do. Mam gets into bed at ten and I take us mugs of cocoa. I sit on the end of the bed, and we sip the cocoa. I talk to her and often get a load of gobbledegook, but I keep talking all the same. And, of course, some nights she's quite lucid and knows what we are discussing.'

I nod and give her the signal to keep talking.

'Then I kissed her forehead as I always do, put out the light, and went back into the lounge to watch TV. I suppose it's like you would do with a child,' she says. 'But let's face it sometimes she is like an infant and has to be totally cared for.'

I sigh and without realising I begin to wring my hands in agitation. I figure it's because I know how it feels as a child not to feel safe and secure. I fight back horrid old memories from when I was little and how scared I had been when my father was in his druggie rage. I'd often crawled under the little table in the kitchen cowering in fear with my hands over my head.

I force my mind back to Liz and ask, 'And this morning – she just wasn't there?'

Liz starts to cry again. Big heaving sobs that seem to wrack her thin chest. 'I took her

morning cuppa in at seven and the bed was
empty. I thought she was in her en-suite
bathroom and ran inside because she has fallen
once in there a few years ago. But it was empty
too.'

'Aah,' I say. 'And I suppose you searched the
other rooms?'

She wipes her hand across and under her drippy
nose then grabs another tissue. 'Yes, of course,
and then I ran outside and searched the garden,
but she was nowhere in sight, so I rang the
police.'

'And did they come straight away?'

Liz shrugs. 'I guess so, but I was panicking too
much and didn't take notice of timing.'

I nod again. My throat feels dry. I get up and
wander over to the water cooler in the corner
and pour two plastic beakers of cold water. I
place them on the coffee table and gulp at mine
relishing the cold liquid in my throat.

'Are both the doors locked at night?' I ask.
'And do you leave the keys in the locks so she
can get out?'

Liz nods miserably. 'I always leave the keys
hanging just in case there's a fire. I figure, if I
was to get trapped in the flames then at least
Mam would be able to get out.'

'Makes good sense,' I say. 'And has Audrey
ever gone out before at night?'

Liz actually leans forward and picks up the
beaker in both her shaking hands and downs half
of the water all at once. 'Nooo, she never has

done - ordinarily she won't even step into the garden unless I'm with her. So, I've never had cause to worry,' she says then fiddles with the chain around her neck. 'Which is the total opposite to what she's always been. Mam changed from being outgoing and loving new places to visit to almost a hermit in the lodge. No matter where I offered to take her, she'd shake her head and tell me she would be scared. But our GP said this was part of the condition. They like familiarity, you, see?'

She pauses then stares at me. 'So, to answer your question - if she does wake through the night, she'll wander around the rooms in a confused state but never outside.'

This is not good, I think and rub my jaw with different scenarios racing through my mind. 'And, was it the back or front door that was open this morning?'

I finish the water and realise that I'm quizzing her which is what the police must have already done but she doesn't seem to mind. I press on trying to build up a picture in my mind.

Liz says, 'It was the back door which leads out into the side garden and faces the wall where the main road is on the other side. But first, she wouldn't be able to scale the wall and second, she hates the noise of the traffic so I can't think she'd willingly leave the caravan park.'

I get up now and begin to pace around the small room thinking through what Liz has said. Why would an old lady suddenly behave totally out of character? I suppose it might be that her condition worsened quickly, but does that happen with Alzheimer's disease? I shrug not knowing the answer.

Liz wails again but louder this time. 'I mean, how can a confused old lady just vanish into thin air? I keep thinking of her lying and shivering in her nighty not knowing where I am – and it's choking me!'

Liz picks at the skin on her thumbnail. 'Maybe someone did see her and took her away – but why? I mean, why would someone take a ninety year old lady?'

She shakes her head in disbelief. I shake mine too agreeing with her that abducting an old lady is not high up on the list of crimes. Young girls, yes, but at Audrey's age what was to be gained from that other than robbery. And, as she was in her nightwear and not carrying a handbag – this was unlikely.

She reaches into her pocket and brings out a packet of cigarettes and lighter. She looks at me with an appealing look on her face as if to ask if I mind.

'It's okay,' I mumble understanding her need to have one because she's in such a state. I can tell her mind is rambling now and is muttering her thoughts more to herself, but I listen carefully to what she is saying.

Liz lights her cigarette and takes a long draw blowing smoke in the opposite direction to me for which I'm grateful. I wander around the back of the room and stare out of the window. I look over towards their small garden and imagine Audrey staggering around confused in the dark. My stomach churns and I frown knowing this is nothing compared to the trauma that Liz is feeling.

She stutters, 'A…and, I was really tired last night – I just crashed out. Although I have a cleaning supervisor, I still like to do spot checks myself on the caravans. So, I choose six vans a week and check toilets, kitchens, and run my fingers along the units looking for dust. There'd been a few issues yesterday because of the high turnover of guests and the bin area wasn't as tidy as I like. There were split rubbish bags which needed to be disposed of and it needed a good sweep, so by the time I sorted all of that out – it was late.'

I smile knowing the high standards set by these two women was how the park looked well-kept and maintained. 'That's understandable, Liz.'

She continues, 'And of course, Mam has no sense of direction so I can't believe she left the caravan park on her own.'

I nod. This makes me think that she's still got to be here somewhere. There's a gentle tap on the door and two middle aged ladies hurry into the room. I can tell they're cleaners because of the blue tabards and I've seen them working around the park.

'Aww, poor, Liz,' one of them cries out.

It's obvious Liz is going to be caught up, so I nod to her then make a hasty retreat.

Chapter Eleven

I stand outside reception deep in thought. I know the police have walked around the park chatting to people, but I can't help thinking that a more extensive search is needed. Audrey could have fallen and rolled underneath one of the caravans or got caught up in bushes on the roadside or paths.

I head back to my caravan and see Amber up ahead with the girls. Thankfully, they're giggling once more, and I call out to her. At the same time, I see Celia and Jim walking down the path towards us in matching blue anoraks although it's not raining now.

Rusty is straining on his lead to get to us and Jim lets him go. He flies past me to the girls who drop down and fuss him. The gigglers are both in pink T-Shirts and shorts and have their hair in bunches with blue ribbons - they look adorable. Rusty is delighted and rolls over barking in glee while they stroke and play with him.

We stop together in a huddle outside the back of my caravan. I explain what Liz has just said and how I'm going to walk around myself to search for Audrey.

Amber chimes in, 'Well, Clive, we'll all help you. We can make it a game of hide and seek, can't we, girls?'

The gigglers jump about excitedly and I catch a fond look in Celia's eyes as she smiles at them. It tells me she would have dearly loved children and I wonder why they didn't have a family. I can also see why Rusty is treated like a baby.

I smile. 'So, I reckon the police will have stuck to the main gravel path that goes in a one-way system around the park,' I say. 'Shall we walk on the grass in between the caravans and look underneath. I'm thinking if Audrey fell, she could have rolled under one of them.'

Jim nods and teases, 'Yes, Sherlock, that's definitely a good idea.'

Celia laughs at this and Jim grins at me now. I'm surprised but pleased to see he's shaken off the earlier grim appearance and miserable outlook.

Flashbacks come into my mind from watching the new editions of Sherlock on TV a few years ago and I chuckle. I can't say that I have any of Benedict Cumberbatch's intelligent traits and powers of deductions, but I pull my shoulders back enjoying the little compliment even if it was said in jest.

Suddenly, the veranda doors open from the caravan facing us. In the three days I've been here I have never seen anyone in there. In fact, I'd thought it was empty. So much for my powers of deduction, I think and smile as a big man about six foot with a stocky build appears. I'm using the word, stocky because he's not fat. Just solid looking in a grey hoodie and long shorts that reach his knees.

'I've just heard about the old lady,' he says. 'And if it's okay, I'd like to offer my assistance.'

I'm quite taken aback. At first, I'd wondered if we had disturbed him, and he was going to complain about the noise we were making.

'Hey, thanks,' I say and automatically hold out my hand to shake. 'I'm, Clive and am staying in the caravan in front of you. And yes please, do join us - as the saying goes, the more the merrier.'

He nods to me and shuffles from one foot to another in brown old-fashioned Jesus sandals. He does, however, take my hand and shake it firmly. I try not to be a wimp at his strong grip and withdraw my hand as soon as possible. Rubbing my stinging knuckles behind my back, I introduce the others and he nods at them all. He doesn't smile, not even at the gigglers – he just nods.

'It's good to meet you all and I'm Dennis. I've been here a few days but have suffered from bad migraines, so I kept the blinds drawn against the strong sun,' he says.

I try to place his accent but don't recognise twangs of North East in his words - there's a mix of other pronunciations. I wouldn't say I was good with accents but can usually distinguish strong drawls like Liverpool, Glasgow, and Birmingham. It's none of these.

He pulls out black sunglasses and places them on his face although the sun isn't shining. The black glasses look stark against his pale face and skin. I figure he's a little older than me, about thirty-five, although the thick, wavy moustache with slight whispers of grey probably makes him look older. I smile to see Amber sizing him up. Does this woman never let up, I think and suppress a chuckle.

'Come along, girls,' she says obviously dismissing him as not up to her standard. 'Shall we start over by the dahlia section, Clive?'

I swing around to her, and she beams at me with that suggestive cocky look in her eye once more. Oh, no, I think, here we go again and look down at the gravel path. Help me please, Celia, I want to beg.

My cheeks flush but I manage to croak, 'Yeah, that'll be great. I'll start off by Liz's lodge and look through the bushes around the back,' I say. 'Maybe, Celia and Jim, you could take the top section of Ash Mews, and Dennis, how about the middle caravans of Millennium Gardens?'

Everyone agrees and Dennis sets off behind us all. Amber takes the girls' hands and moves forwards. I walk past Celia while Jim is putting the lead back onto Rusty. I can't help ruffling his ears as I pass by - he's such a gorgeous dog.

Jim pulls back his shoulders and says, 'Well, if anyone can sniff out the old lady it'll be Rusty here because he's got Spaniel in his breed, and they're well known for hunting.'

I nod. While I say good bye, Celia tugs at my jacket sleeve and whispers to me, 'Dennis must have been listening to what we were saying from inside his caravan or how else would have known about Audrey being missing - I think he's a weirdo!'

I tut and then sigh while setting off to walk. I don't like to see people being victimised just because they're different. And yes, I figure Dennis doesn't look or sound run-of-the-mill but that doesn't mean to say he is weird. The man has offered to help in the search therefore he must have a sense of decency and purpose. And although he is a stranger to us it doesn't mean he's not a good person. I shake my head thinking of Celia and her narrow-mindedness.

The caravans aren't set out in exact rows. Some of the backs and fronts of the caravans jut-out in angles and are in different colours of cream, white, and pale green. The grass in between them all is neatly trimmed, and I've seen the groundsmen out with lawnmowers a few times since I arrived. This makes it easier to look underneath which I do moving forwards.

All the roofs are the same however, and the seagulls are squawking and running along the tops making an almighty racket. I can see how they get a bad press at the coastal areas with signs up requesting holiday makers not to feed them.

Apparently, they can be quite vicious when snatching food from hands. I remember reading that in Whitby the usual low-backed benches facing the harbour are being replaced with high backs to stop the seagulls sweeping down on people from behind and catching them unawares whilst eating their fish and chips. This is a good idea, I reckon while stooping and looking underneath the caravans as I head over towards the big lodge.

The park seems busier today with many more families around. In the largest section where the caravans don't have verandas, I see families sitting outside on loungers and deck chairs sunning themselves. Bottles of wine and cans of lager stand on small picnic tables. There's a good mix of grandparents, adults, children and in other places groups of young men and women which look like hen and stag parties. When I come to the end row of the caravans, I see two families with small BBQs outside and men grilling burgers and sausages. There's a real holiday vibe about them all as they take in the much needed fresh air, sunshine, and relaxation. Everyone looks happy and contented which I know at any other time would please Liz.

When I reach the lodge, I scour the bushes and garden, around and inside the perimeter fence. I figure Liz won't mind me doing this. Where can Audrey have got to, I think as suddenly the sun makes an appearance. I look up to the blue sky once more and frown.

How far could a lady of her age walk? And especially in the dark? The park has lamp posts on most corners and the caravans have small outside lights on their boardings, but still, it would be difficult to negotiate the paths at night.

I suppose it depends upon exactly what time Audrey left their lodge. If it had been midnight then some of the revellers from the pub and restaurant might have been straggling back to their caravans, but if it was three in the morning then nobody would be around to see her lost and alone. My gut twists when I think of the poor old lady and remember my own Gran while I'm searching.

Although I was too young to understand death and what it entailed when Gran died, I remember crying for weeks afterwards. My mum had been drunker than usual and didn't even make it to the funeral – she couldn't stand up that day, but kept chanting, 'The dragon of a mother-in-law died of cancer – Ha!'

I didn't think Gran was a dragon because I missed her so much. My father had gone off on a bender with his druggie pals and stayed away for a whole month. He only came back to see if his mother had left any money.

I stop at the caravan park entrance and lean against the huge wide sign. One of the reception staff is standing at the mini roundabout directing guests who are arriving at 4pm. She points to where their caravans are based on the park and hands out a map.

I sigh as my thoughts return to Gran and how her neighbour came to take me to the funeral. There'd only been a handful of people sitting on two pews in the church. I hadn't really understood back then but I know now she should have had so much more. The priest had organised everything and I presume that the funeral had been paid for by the church. I'd felt my world was caving-in on me because I had known I would be totally on my own.

There should have been flowers and people saying nice words about her because she had been kind, especially to me. I kick at a nearby lamp post in temper and frustration at my parents. Old people should be cared for and cherished like Audrey is by Liz. In my eyes I see it as pay-back time for all the years of love and attention they've given us. And, if Gran hadn't died so early, I would have been able to do that for her. I swallow hard and feel my eyes water.

I didn't even know I had a grandfather until I met Barbie and we went through a folder of old documents which had been given to me when I was in the young offenders' institution. I hadn't looked at these since my day of release. Barbie and I discovered that my mother had died of alcoholic poisoning. Maybe, I had been told in the institution, but aged fifteen, it hadn't registered with me.

'This is all I have left of my childhood,' I'd told Barbie. 'And I don't know to this day if my father is actually still alive?'

When I had opened the folder, a card dropped to the floor, and we read it together.

'Oh, it's a baby boy congratulation card,' she'd said.

I had read aloud the verse and greetings from Mum and Dad. When I pushed the card back into the folder, Barbie noticed the small writing on the back. Clive and Nancy McPherson with an address in Edinburgh.

'What??' I'd shrieked. 'Jeez, all the years I've had this and never looked at the back of the card? Well, there's a thing - I'm half Scottish.'

We'd set off together to Edinburgh for Hogmanay and after hours of tracing we had found my grandfather in an old people's home.

I smile now remembering the three visits we've made and although he is weak with a chronic chest ailment, I love to spend time with him. He tells me great tales about old times in Edinburgh. I purse my lips knowing that when he does pass, he'll have everything at his funeral that he deserves.

I hear my name being called and spin around to see Celia, Jim, and another four people heading towards me. I wipe a hand over my damp eyes, pull back my shoulders and stride towards them.

Celia and Jim are carrying their blue anoraks now but two of their friends have identical green jackets. Oh, really, I think and bite the inside of my cheek to stop from hooting in laughter.

'Hey, Clive,' Jim calls with his palms open and shaking his head as if to say we've drawn a blank. 'There's no sign of her anywhere…'

I nod and am introduced to their friends. I recognise the faces from around our caravans in

Ash Mews and wonder if they are part of Celia's gin and tonic brigade.

  We discuss the situation and Celia tells me that Amber hasn't seen anything of Audrey, so she has taken the girls down to the causeway. I nod and we walk slowly back to Ash Mews.

Chapter Twelve

Amber

'Come on, girls,' she calls out. 'Let's go down towards the lighthouse for a walk.'

Amber takes them by the hand and heads to the main entrance of the caravan park. The sun has just come out again and although there's a slight sea breeze, she reckons a run around might wear them out, so they'll sleep well tonight.

They'd played hide and seek looking for Audrey which the girls had loved but as the old lady was nowhere to be seen they had soon tired of the game. All three of them had started off calling the lady's name, 'Audrey! Audrey, where are you?' But Amber could tell the game soon wore thin when nothing happened.

On the other side of the pavement, she spots Clive leaning against the caravan park sign and even at a distance she can tell he looks forlorn. She wonders what's happened and why he looks downhearted? Maybe he knows the family and that's why he seems so upset about Audrey.

Amber shouts across, 'Hey, Clive, there's no sign of Audrey, so I'm going to take the girls down to the causeway and let them run around on the grass.'

She sees Clive wave and give her a thumbs-up sign. He's so nice, she thinks walking on the path down the main road holding the girls' hands. But a relationship with Clive would never

*work even if he was interested which Amber
didn't think he was. She was tied up, in more
ways than one.*

*Even if she was free from Kieran, which she
wasn't, who on earth would take on a single
mother with two small girls to raise? Amber
knew if she said this to her mum the reply would
be, 'Another divorced man with kids and then
you'll end up with a big happy family.'*

*And that sounded lovely. It wasn't that she
didn't appreciate Mum's eternal optimism and
faith in her, but for some reason, Amber's life
never turned out smelling of roses. It did for
other women but just not for her.*

*Jayden tugs on her hand and she looks down at
her sweet little face. This morning hadn't been
easy being cooped up in the caravan and she felt
bad for running out of patience. They were both
such live-wires, Amber grinned, but knew she
shouldn't complain. The girls were exactly the
same as she'd been at their age.*

*She had snapped at Jayden near the slot
machines and now Amber wanted to make up for
this by being extra nice. She wanted them to
have the best holiday ever and frowned, God
knew when she would ever be able to give them
another.*

*'What was that, Jayden?' She asked and bent
down to listen while stroking her hair.*

*Her daughter asked, 'I wonder why Audrey
would leave Liz and the caravans because it's
such a nice place to live?'*

Amber smiled. Oh, the age of innocence, she thought and began to swing their hands backwards and forwards. 'Well,' she replied. 'I don't think she wanted to leave but got a little confused during the night and lost her way.'

They reach the mini-roundabout and cross over the road. Amber lets go of their hands and they take off. They run down onto the grass verge and swing from the railings laughing and doing cartwheels. Amber knows they're far enough away from the traffic pulling into the car park, but she keeps to the edge until they reach the slope down towards the causeway.

Amber can see the tide is in, so they won't be able to walk the short distance over the causeway, but at least they're outside and the sun is shining again. She calls to the girls who run back up to her side.

'Okay, so we won't be able to go into the lighthouse today but maybe tomorrow morning when the tide is out,' she says.

Gabrielle looks up at her and asks, 'How deep is it because we can both swim?'

Amber throws her head back and laughs. 'Er, no, it's quite shallow but you aren't ruining those sandals your nana bought for you.'

Massive old rocks are in a zig-zag row down the other side of the railings, and she warns the girls to take care. She takes both their hands and stands still looking at the brilliant white tower of the lighthouse. It is simply an amazing sight and pulls out her mobile to send a photo to her mum.

The old path leading to the causeway is cracked in places and they all watch mesmerised at the gentle waves which lap into the small rockpools.

A Chinese couple are having their photograph taken with their backs facing the sea and the lighthouse, so Gabrielle and Jayden stand still until they are finished. Amber smiles at their good conduct knowing, although she has done her best to raise them with the strong family values she was taught, much of their behaviour is down to her mum.

All of a sudden, Gabrielle cries, 'She's there!'

Amber turns to where her finger is pointing. She looks down to her right where there are four very old stone steps flanked by a dark, pebble-dashed wall. The steps lead down into the waves.

Amber sees Audrey's head on the last step. Her grey hair is splayed out in the frothy sea water and tangled with seaweed floating in the sea. Her head is lolled back but the rest of her body is in the deeper water.

OMG, she thinks, it's Audrey and she's dead. Amber can't stop herself from screaming. The Chinese couple spin around and two youngish men hurry towards her and the girls. They all stand staring as though none of them can quite believe what they are seeing.

Amber can feel Jayden's hand in hers shaking which snaps her back into action. The children shouldn't see this, and Amber knows she has to hold it together for their sakes. She turns the

*girls around and begins to pull them away from
the sight of Audrey. She hears one of the men
shouting in his mobile asking for the police and
ambulance.*

*Amber touches his arm, and says, 'The police
are up at the caravan park – the old lady has
been missing all day.'*

*He nods and relays the information while
Amber hurries the girls back up the path and
slumps down with them on the grass verge. She
draws her knees up to her chest and puts her
head down. She cuddles both girls' into her side
hoping they won't be traumatised by what
they've seen.*

*Jayden asks, 'Mum, has Audrey fallen asleep
down there in the sea?'*

*Amber begins to tremble. What on earth will
she tell them? Should she use the word death
and explain that she has drowned? Oh, God, she
wished Mum was here.*

Chapter Thirteen

It's only when I'm back in the caravan that I realise I've not had a drink since this morning and am gasping for a coffee. I open the fridge door and pick out the empty milk carton. Damn, I curse and then smile knowing it drives Barbie mad when I do this. My wallet is in the back pocket of my jeans, and I hurry down to the shop to buy milk.

When I turn the corner, I hear all the commotion. The blonde policewoman is outside reception shouting into her phone and another young officer is hurrying Liz out of the main doors.

Liz's hair is flying about in the breeze. She turns and sees me, so I hurry up to her.

Liz shouts, 'Oh, Clive, they've found her!' She pulls the thin strap of her shoulder bag over her head slotting it across her chest. 'W…will you come with me?'

I run up the path towards her and can't help hugging her. 'Hey, that's great news!'

However, the look on the policewoman's face alerts me to the fact that this is not good news. She shakes her head and I feel my stomach slump.

'Liz,' I say. 'Let's take it slowly because we don't know what's happened and I think we should prepare ourselves for a shock.'

I see the policewoman nod at me as if to say good job and I climb into the back of the police car with Liz.

The policewoman says, 'We have asked Ms Mathews to remain here until we ascertain exactly what has happened, but she is refusing.'

Liz takes my hand and squeezes it tightly. 'I heard the call on the other policeman's phone saying she is down at the causeway, so I've told them they can either take me or I'll run down there myself!'

The policewoman starts the engine and I feel my heart begin to pound. Liz is struggling to fasten her seat because her hands are shaking. I click it into place for her and fasten mine as we tear off through the main entrance.

The blue lights on the police car are flashing and the noise seems to be deafening when the policewoman pulls straight out and down to the mini-roundabout. I can see all the hullabaloo up ahead before we even reach the car park and know from watching and writing my own crime stories that this doesn't look good at all.

The car park is busy. Another two police officers are pulling tape in blue and white stating, POLICE DO NOT CROSS, around the whole of the area and instructing drivers to reverse and turn around out of the car park.

A crowd has gathered on the other side of the taped area which makes me scowl. What is it they want to see? I read somewhere about accident or suicide tourists. These are people who mill around longing to see dead bodies or traumatic events. I think this is ghoulish and know I wouldn't be interested to see the remains of an old woman's dead body. But obviously these people do because now I've seen this scene - I know Audrey is dead.

It amazes me how quickly bad news spreads so fast but nowadays it is because of social media. I can see the crowd holding up their smart phones trying to get closer photographs and know there'll be images of the causeway and the barriers already on Facebook and Twitter. What is it that interests people in tragedy and accidents? It's a well-known fact that drivers often cause more mayhem when they slow down to stare at road traffic accidents.

I look ahead at the sea and remember how cold it was when I waded through it up to my ankles. Audrey would have to be superhuman to survive for any length of time in that temperature. The policewoman slows down and drives a little way along the narrow road to the start of the causeway path.

Liz is swearing and fumbling trying to undo her seatbelt which is entwined with the strap of her shoulder bag.

The policewoman says, 'Please, Ms Mathews just stay in the car until I come back and find out what's happened.'

Liz almost growls. 'My name is Liz, and I'm not staying anywhere – I have to see her!'

I hear the policewoman tut, but I help Liz with the belt, and we climb out of the back of the car together.

Liz starts to run, and I keep up with her calling all the while, 'Liz, wait! Please just slow down!'

But there's no stopping her and my heart is pounding as I hurry alongside and down the path. Another length of police tape is across the top of four old steps on the side of the causeway path. An older police sergeant is standing guard with his back to the sea, however, his torso fills most of the opening to the top step.

'Hey,' he shouts, 'You can't go down there.'

Liz swears at him and then cries, 'I'm her daughter and I have to be with her!'

He is short and broad but holds her arm firmly. I can tell he's not hurting her although she's struggling against him like a wild cat. He stands to the side still holding onto Liz. And that's when I hear her howl like an animal at the sight before us.

I don't mind admitting that my legs feel like jelly and my knees begin to knock. Although I have written about dead bodies, I've never actually seen one. I swallow hard as bile rises up in my throat.

Audrey's head is lolled back on the top step. She looks almost ethereal with a white, blotchy, puffed-up face. From what I remember she had a thin craggy face - now it seems twice the size. Her eyes are half open as if she is looking down to the sea, and her lips are huge and pale blue. There are bits of seaweed tangled in her hair which has come out of the tight bun she'd had when I met her.

Liz sobs and pleads with the sergeant. 'But I just want to sit on the step and cuddle her?'

I can see him melt a little and loosen his hold on her arm. 'Sorry, pet, but we can't let you. It's what we call a crime scene, and no one is allowed down there until my boss arrives with the coroner.'

Licking my dry lips, I try to explain how our feet might contaminate the scene and, how we can't touch anything especially not Audrey. I see Liz's knees buckle as huge racking sobs escape from her mouth. I take her other arm and between me and the sergeant we catch her before she falls to the ground.

Once again, I'm reminded of my imaginary detective in Durham and shake my head. Jeez, I'd thought I would be doing a lot of things on my caravan holiday but living in my own written story wasn't one of them.

'Please come and sit down, Liz,' I say. 'There's nothing we can do here – we have to let the police do their jobs.'

Her body flops against my chest and I put both my arms around her. This time she lets me lead her away to the grass behind the railings. I ease her down and sit next to her with my arms tightly around her while she sobs into my T-shirt.

'Oh, Clive, she's dead,' Liz cries. 'I'd hoped, well, I didn't know what to think, but I…I'd prayed I could at least have a few minutes with her.'

I rock her gently back and forth not knowing how to cope with the situation and decide by doing this I'm trying to console myself too. I feel crushingly disappointed because I too had hoped we'd be able to find Audrey alive. I only pray she didn't suffer too much and, if she was having what Liz called, one of her off days, she wouldn't have known anything about falling into the sea. That is, of course, if she did fall in, I think and stare across at the gentle waves lapping on the rocks.

'I know, I know,' I keep repeating to her because I don't know what else to say.

My heart begins to slow again, and I feel Liz's body stop trembling. I look around at the scene unfolding with police cars and officers coming and going out of the taped area. The sun is still shining, and I reckon it all looks a bit grotesque. It would be bad enough to happen on any day, but on a warm summer's day with the seafront full of happy holidaymakers it seems a hundred times worse for some reason.

She sniffs loudly. 'I mean, h…how in God's name has she got down here, Clive?'

I shake my head. 'I don't know, Liz. I know you've already said she couldn't walk very far.' I say drawing my eyebrows together and pausing for breath. 'But maybe she had managed in her confused state?'

Liz pulls away from my T-shirt which I can feel is now sodden, but it doesn't matter. She shakes her head in dispute, sits up, and pulls a tissue from the shoulder bag to wipe her face.

My brain kicks in again, and ask, 'Did she know the way down here?'

Liz tuts. 'Of course, she does we've lived here for over sixty years and Mam would often walk down to the lighthouse and seafront. She'd wander about for hours. However, that was years ago,' she says. 'Lately, she's struggled to walk around our little garden let alone reach the main entrance.'

I turn and look behind to see a Chinese couple and Amber standing on the grass verge. She is holding the gigglers' hands. I sigh knowing they won't be giggling now and wonder if they've heard about Audrey and, what's happened.

I hope the girls weren't anywhere near the rockpools when Audrey was discovered because it would be a haunting sight for them to have fixed in their memories. I've a few hauntings of my own from being little and shiver with recollections of my mum with a cut lip and her screams when my father was in one of his rages and beat her. Looking back now, I wished I hadn't seen and heard all that I did – it certainly left its mark in my mind.

A small white van is allowed through the tape after showing ID cards to the police officers and pulls up as near to the causeway path as possible. I watch two men get out carrying large silver metal cases which look like they could hold equipment. They pull on white protective clothing over their jeans and sweatshirts, and then overshoes on top of their boots while a tent is being erected. Stupidly, I recall the TV shows I've watched and figure this is the coroner's team or indeed, it could be the coroner himself.

I notice that Liz is watching them too and I explain. 'I think it's the coroner's team who are responsible for collecting personal belongings for evidence, examining the scene to find out what's happened and then Audrey will be taken to a morgue facility somewhere for a post mortem, which of course, will establish her cause of death,' I say. 'Whether it be, an accident, suicide or unexplained.'

Liz nods. 'Yeah, Vera used to be Mam's favourite show on TV,' she said. 'God, that was a stupid thing to say when she's just died!'

I shake my head. 'It's not, Liz. If you feel the need to talk about your mam, then that's fine – go ahead it might make you feel better.'

She nods. 'And, I still watch the repeats of Vera on channel ten because they're all filmed along our coastline and up into Northumberland.'

I smile and can tell Liz has settled in her thoughts now. Gone is the blind panic and hysteria which she's been showing and feeling. I frown knowing death does this to a person - it's a type of acceptance. Although it's been traumatic for Liz racing down here and seeing Audrey, I can tell it has quelled all of the frenetic questions that must have raced through her mind since this morning. Is she still alive? Where is she? What's happening? If we can find her in time, we might save her?

Now Liz is here at the scene and can see for herself that Audrey is dead and has left our world, those thoughts no longer exist. They'll be replaced by thousands of other questions, but they'll be more controlled thoughts because timing is no longer of the essence. Liz knows there's nothing more she can do to help Audrey because she's passed.

Liz seems much calmer and sits hugging her knees like a teenager.

Two seagulls up above squark together and I look upwards at the noise, but Liz doesn't flinch. I suppose when you've lived at the coast all of your life it's something you get so used to hearing it doesn't register as out of the ordinary anymore. I rub her back. 'Are you feeling any better?'

She nods and takes my hand. 'Thanks, Clive, I know you're a stranger really and I've only just met you, but thanks a million – you've been a great help.'

I feel tears choke my throat and swallow hard. I've always struggled with compliments and gratitude although I don't know why. Barbie reckons it's because I never had any praise or encouragement growing up, so as an adult it's new to me. I reckon she could be right.

Last year when I'd helped our neighbourhood watch community in York deal with burglaries and tracking down a pick-pocketing gang, I struggled to cope with their gratitude afterwards. Which is strange because I love to have recognition and praise in reviews of my novel. But here with Liz, in this sort of close-knit relationship, I don't know how to handle myself.

My cheeks flush and my mouth dries. 'Aww, it's okay, Liz, I've just done what anyone else would have done.'

She abruptly shakes her head. 'Oh, no, you've done so much more. The cleaners told me how you had a group of holidaymakers searching underneath the caravans and you trawled our garden areas near the roadside which is more than the police did. And that's apart from sitting with me yesterday and then racing down here,' she says sighing heavily. 'I'd h…hate to be sitting here on my own.'

Chapter Fourteen

I look back up the road and spot an unmarked police car arrive. An oldish man climbs out and I watch him talk to the police officers and the sergeant at the steps. By the way the young police officers act and their body-language, I reckon this is the boss. He's wearing an old type of parker jacket and has his hands thrust deep inside the pockets while he struts about looking at the causeway, the path, and bends down on his hunkers to stare at Audrey.

'I think that's an inspector or at least the guy who is in charge of the case,' I say and look sideways at Liz. She too, is staring at him and nods in agreement but doesn't speak.

The blonde policewoman approaches him, and he stands back up to talk to her. I can tell he is listening then swings around to face us as she points in our direction. I watch him stride towards us and we both scramble to our feet.

The man isn't tall but has an authoritative air as he nears us with the policewoman trailing in his footsteps. He's wearing what look like well-worn corduroy trousers and old brogues that have seen better days. I reckon he's late-fifties and is supporting what we know locally as a Bobby Charlton look. He's nearly bald but has a long strand of hair across the front of his head.

He holds out his hand to Liz and says, 'I'm Detective Inspector Ted Barker and will be dealing with what's happened to your mother.'

She takes his hand to shake and then he turns to me. 'And you are?'

Liz says, 'He's one of our customers at the caravan park who has been helping me.'

Ted nods and runs his hand over the thin strand of hair that is now flapping in the sea breeze. I'm thinking he should have some gel on this, or as my granddad would use, a pot of Brylcreem – it would certainly keep it in one place.

'Well, Ms Mathews, I'm sorry to see and hear about your mam's passing, but rest assured I'll do all I can to find out exactly what's happened to her and will keep you informed every step of the way.'

Liz and I both nod. I look at her to see if she is going to ask any questions. Liz doesn't appear to, so I ask, 'And when will you have any findings, Inspector?'

Ted looks me up and down. I can't help my back shivering a little as if I am under some type of scrutiny. It takes me back to my early days of juvenile crime and the young persons' institution when I was often under suspicion. Although by that stage I was totally innocent of all misdemeanours. I suppose the feelings of guilt and wrongdoing never leave a person - at least they haven't in my case.

I shake this off and pull my shoulders back knowing I am totally innocent and have nothing to fear.

'It'll take as long as it takes,' he says.

I look directly into his small beady eyes. He seems to realise that his answer sounds abrupt and continues, 'We'll try to be as quick as possible, and my police officers will be talking to people on the caravan park to see if they can shed any light on the event.'

That's better, I think and smile at him. I receive nothing back just a blank stare. What I can smell is a waft of Old Spice aftershave and want to smile at the comparison to my granddad. Although, of course, Ted isn't as old as him. I wipe the smile from my face and look down at the gravel path knowing the situation is serious and is unravelling before our eyes.

He turns to Liz again and adds, 'Ms Mathews, is it possible that your mother could have taken her own life, or has she ever expressed suicidal thoughts?'

I gasp. What a question to ask at a time like this, I rage and automatically want to challenge him. However, I recall how detectives have to ask awkward questions as soon as possible to ascertain the facts and hold my tongue.

I can feel the anger coming from Liz in waves. She narrows her eyes and cries, 'Are you taking the piss? Mam doesn't know what day of the week it is, or sometimes even her own name – she's not capable of such rational thoughts!'

Ted looks affronted at her outburst and puffs out his chubby cheeks. I know Liz's eruption is because she's hurt and distraught - it's not a personal attack on him. So, if I can see this why can't he?

He bristles and gives a small cough. 'Okay, Ms Mathews, I have to ask these questions in an unexplained death in a public place, but I think that it would be best for you to go back to your caravan now and like I say, we'll be in touch.'

She stiffens. 'First, we don't live in a caravan. Mam and I live in a lodge, and we own the caravan park. And second, I'm not going anywhere as long as my mam is lying down there. I'll stay here to keep out of your way as instructed,' she says and snorts at the policewoman. 'But I will be here until they take Mam to the mortuary. I won't leave her alone down there in the sea.'

Ted nods and turns away calling over his shoulder. 'As you wish.'

We sit together and Liz delves into her shoulder bag. She pulls out her cigarettes and a packet of chewing gum then offers me a piece.

I take it gratefully because my mouth is dry, and I have the beginnings of a headache. Her face is white now and nearly as white as Audrey's had been. Her hands tremble as she lights the cigarette and I know it's the shock – I feel so sorry for her.

Liz mutters, 'He's a right old git – isn't he?'

Although I agree, the last thing Liz needs now is concern over the handling of Audrey's death. It was the first dead body I've seen but reckon it won't be the first Ted has dealt with. I bet he's seen loads of bodies during his long years of service which makes me wonder, is Audrey just another corpse to him? I must admit it's the impression he's given us both.

I think quickly and reply, 'Maybe, but sometimes old is good because he'll have loads of experience which the younger ones won't.'

We watch the comings and goings and the forensic team during which time Liz alternates between gentle sobbing, wiping her nose and smoking cigarettes.

Eventually they leave and an unmarked van with darkened windows arrives. However, we can't see them retrieve Audrey from the sea because of the tent. This, I figure is good because Liz will no doubt see Audrey in the funeral parlour where her mam will look a lot better than she does now. And Liz may have to identify Audrey in the mortuary later today or tomorrow.

Liz stands up when the van sets off slowly and I scramble up next to her. My knees have nearly seized up and I relish the short walk ahead. The van with Audrey inside passes by slowly and I see Liz's hands grip the railings until her knuckles are white. She starts to cry again and sobs, 'Aww, Mam, I'm so s…sorry I wasn't with you.'

I'm not sure whether the driver deliberately goes at a slow speed out of respect for Audrey and Liz, but I put my arm along her shoulder, and we start to walk behind the van up the road.

The crowd has disappeared, and we continue over and across the roundabout after the van turns left.

Liz says, 'I'm pleased they're taking Mam along the seafront for the last time – she's always loved living here.'

I nod and look back. 'Yep, you're fortunate – it's a fantastic place to live.'

In silence we reach the small picket fence around her lodge, and she stops still. Liz traces her finger along their plaque over the name, Audrey and bows her head looking down at the grass. It's as though she's dreading going back inside alone. I take her mobile and add my number so she can ring if I'm needed.

'Come on,' I say. 'We both need a hot cup of tea.'

We enter her lodge by the front door and see one of the cleaners in the hall who offers to stay with Liz and hugs her tightly. The cleaner tells us that the whole caravan park is abuzz with the news.

Chapter Fifteen

I hadn't been able to sleep last night. I'd rang Barbie and told her all about finding Audrey and what had happened whilst drinking three glasses of water and two cups of coffee because I had been so thirsty. Which of course had meant I was up twice to use the bathroom during the night. I'd tossed and turned with the image of Audrey coming into my dreams and felt quite claustrophobic in the small bedroom as opposed to our large airy room at home.

Not sleeping well would have been unusual for me before I met Barbie as I've always been a good sleeper. I'd found it easy to empty my mind after reading for a while. But since we met, I only have a deep sleep when she is curled up next to me and I know she's safe.

Now I'm up early wanting to get out of the caravan and find some fresh air and open space. I stand in the tiny shower cubicle feeling claustrophobic again and let the hot water beat down on my head. I'm longing for our big bathroom at home with the high ceiling and room to manoeuvre while washing my hair.

After a huge breakfast, I dump the crockery in the sink alongside dishes from yesterday. I know Barbie would be riding my case but shrug and throw empty packets into the black rubbish bag deciding to clean up later.

I set off to walk without a plan in mind and find myself wandering back down to the causeway. I stride out and breathe in big lungsful of fresh sea air. I'm hoping to check for peace of mind that yesterday did actually happen and it hadn't been a figment of my imagination and not just a dream.

The tide is out, and the causeway is open. There is no one about and the car park is empty. Probably the holidaymakers are all still in hotels and guest houses eating breakfast and haven't ventured out as yet. It's a beautiful morning and the seagulls seem to be squawking in unison.

I stand at the top of the steps which are all visible now that the sea isn't lapping up onto them. It's as though none of yesterday happened and Audrey hadn't even been there. Of course, the police, their tape and tent are long gone and it's very quiet. Spooky even, I think feeling the eerie sensation run up my back.

I remember my instinct the day I'd arrived into their reception and knew either something harmful had happened in that room or something bad was going to happen. Although, I nod, the really bad thing hadn't been in there - it was down here. But, feeling justified, I figure that Audrey had been in the reception room on that day when I'd experienced the uneasy vibes.

Looking down at the steps, I remember the sight of Audrey's head on the top and shudder. The poor old lady had really suffered dying in the sea unless of course she was already dead when she went under. I hunch down on bended knees and look at the grey battered old steps. Of course, the forensic team will have gone over the place with a fine comb, and I don't expect to see anything they haven't, but I figure it's worth a look anyway.

I've always gone on my instinct in situations and I'm a great believer in fate. Look how I met Barbie wandering through The Shambles. If it hadn't been for the shopping bag splitting and my tins of baked beans rolling down the kerb, she wouldn't have stopped to help. Barbie would have passed me by without a second glance. I smile, the gods had been with me that day and hopefully they'll pay me a visit today.

I shake myself back to the here and now and wonder how Audrey did end up on the steps? This was one of the questions that had tormented me during the night when sleep eluded, and I'd thrashed around the bed. And the other query was – did she actually manage to walk down here? Although Liz thought that was out of the question, if she had got here on foot then perhaps Audrey fell on the top step, banged her head, and slid under the water.

Or had somebody spotted her coming out of the main entrance, given her a lift down here and she'd managed to stagger down the path leading to the causeway. But who would do that to an old lady wearing a nightdress? Surely, a responsible person would alert the police or hospital as to how they'd found her wandering around? I know I would. I suppose, a member of the general public could have felt they were doing Audrey a favour by giving her a lift in their car although I think this highly unlikely.

I force myself to remember her exact image yesterday. Her grey hair had been floating in the water and I know with certainty that there'd been no sign of any blood if she had banged her head. However, if she had lain here for a while then the sea could have washed blood away. I frown, this will be something Liz could find out today because usually there's a preliminary report as to the cause of death and timing.

I get up, shake down my jogger bottoms over my trainers and meander over the rocky causeway staring at the sea which is far out behind the lighthouse. The different colours of blue and black with gentle bubbly waves are mesmerising and it cheers me to see this. In and out with such a rhythmic motion that it makes me feel settled somehow as if all is well, which basically, it isn't.

I check my watch to see that it is nine thirty and know once inside the historic centre I'll be able to find out what time the tides were low yesterday. And on the previous night. Walking over the causeway, I look across at the mossy rockpools on either side with puddles of sea water and small areas of sand. These look slippery and I wonder - if Audrey had made it to this area and tumbled down, did she drag herself in a dazed state across to the steps?

On the island, I reach a flight of white stone steps and at the top walk onto a grassy area which is surrounded with white walls. There's a cottage with a red roof to my left with two cars parked. I wonder who lives here and look behind to see the two low white buildings which is my view from the caravan. This is sign-posted as the café and historic centre.

I enter the centre and begin to look around. The information is useful. I learn that the tide yesterday came in at 1.15pm which was around the time when Audrey had been found and we were down here. And, on the previous night the tide was out at 6pm and came in again at 1am. Therefore, if Audrey had wandered down and fell on the steps it had to be before one o'clock in the morning.

I hear two members of staff chatting in the corner behind a screen agog about what had happened yesterday with Audrey.

A male voice said, 'Poor old soul must have wandered down here and drowned in the sea.'

Then an older female voice replied, 'Yes, but technically speaking we can't say she died on the island because it was on the old steps which are on the mainland.'

I muse, there's obviously a certain pride and definition between islanders and mainlanders here. Which is a little like borders and rivers that separate areas. The river divides Newcastle and Northumberland from County Durham and Sunderland with rivalry between the locals who live in the two areas. Especially the football teams.

So, probably when I get back to the caravan park it'll be the same and they'll be saying Audrey died on the mainland. I think of the adage, news travels fast and nod to myself.

Apparently, according to the information in the historic centre the first light here was from an 11th-century monastic chapel. The monks kept a lantern on the tower to warn passing ships of the danger on the rocks and then a lighthouse was built in 1664 using stone from the priory. This was demolished when the current lighthouse and adjacent keepers' cottages were built in 1898 by the John Miller company. The lighthouse was decommissioned in 1984 which was two years after its conversion to automatic operation.

I note that it's possible to climb the 137 steps on a spiral staircase to the top of the lighthouse for the most spectacular views of the North East coastline. However, it says, if you cannot manage the steps, a video facility allows you to experience the same views in colour at ground level.

I decide upon the video and grin knowing my get fit regime hasn't lasted long. I find out that amazingly the red roof cottage with limited access times because of the tide had been put up for sale in June 2011 for £425,000.

I whistle through my teeth - how cool would it be to live here? I consider the limitations of the causeway and shake my head. The details tell me that the cottage is steeped in history with 19th Century graffiti on the windowsills and gunshots in some of the doors. I sigh and then ponder - would you really want hundreds of tourists trailing around your garden and cottage all year round? And, even if it was branded a once in a lifetime opportunity, it wouldn't suit me and Barbie.

I read how the lighthouse is also used as a signal for airline pilots flying towards Newcastle Airport where they turn towards the mainland. Smiling I remember how years ago when we flew back from Spain, I'd noticed the white tower but hadn't realised it was St. Mary's.

More information tells me that it is difficult to imagine such a small and tranquil island could have a dark secret and at once my antennae is on red alert. It had been the setting of a horrific and brutal murder by smugglers of a man named, Anthony Mitchell. In the nineteenth century a local couple opened a pub known as The Square and Compass, and although lived peacefully there for decades they were eventually evicted in a dispute over their drunken customers brawling on neighbouring land. Both the family and their pigs were chucked off the island. I hoot to myself thinking about the pigs.

Retracing my steps back over the causeway I think all the way about the sea. Now that I know the tide timings it's easy to figure out when Audrey was engulfed with water on the steps. Maybe the most straightforward answer is that she simply waded down the steps into the sea in a confused state not aware of what she was doing. I believe this is likely with dementia sufferers because they don't have awareness of their surroundings or sensory feelings. They can't distinguish between hot or cold, whether they are full or hungry, in pain or comfortable.

However, the complicated answer is that Audrey had been taken to the steps by someone and left there when the tide was out. And if she hadn't been alone, to use the old saying, did she fall or was she pushed?

I shake my head knowing Jim is right. When you have an inquisitive mind, it tends to run riot. I decide things like this only happen in fiction and not in real life, especially not in a caravan park in Whitley Bay.

Chapter Sixteen

I walk back through the main entrance and see two groundsmen standing together talking. Further up the main path are three young cleaners with black sacks chatting and I reckon they're all discussing Audrey's death. On my way back along Ashley Mews, I pass two dog walkers of which the man calls out, 'Awful news, isn't it?'

I simply nod and continue up the path. At the back of my caravan, I see Amber standing at her side door.

'Hey, there,' I say. She is still in pink fluffy pyjamas and huge floppy slippers with dog heads on them. She looks tired. The sun is on the front veranda therefore the side of the caravan is shaded which seems to heighten her dull eyes and face.

'Hi, Clive,' she says cradling a mug of coffee in her hands as though gaining comfort from the warmth. 'Wasn't yesterday a horrible day?'

I look behind her for the gigglers but they're nowhere to be seen. Amber must realise that I'm looking for them. 'The girls are still in bed,' she says. 'None of us had much sleep last night.'

I nod. 'Me, neither. I tossed and turned most of the night, so I've been for a walk to try and clear my head.'

Amber sniffs and I see her huge oval eyes moisten. She tells me her account of how they'd spotted Audrey and I gasp. Also, how a Chinese couple rang the police and because they were witnesses, they've given their contact details and a statement to the police.

Dear, Lord, I think, those poor little girls seeing an awful sight like that. It spooked me enough and I'm an adult who understands death, but the girls won't. I rub my chin feeling so sorry for them all and tell her this.

She inhales a deep breath as if to fight back tears. 'I'm afraid I didn't behave very well and screamed when I saw the old woman's face in the sea – it was horrible!' she says. 'Which scared the girls even more before I dragged them away.'

'Ooh, Amber,' I say. 'That's more than understandable because you'd had a shock – don't beat yourself up about it because you realised in time and got them out of eyesight.'

She pulls her shoulders back a little and nods. 'I've been up twice with Jayden my youngest because she was having bad dreams.'

Amber looks at me directly but there's no suggestive tone now in either her voice or eyes. It's not the time to be flirting and for this I'm grateful. I can see the worry and turmoil twisting in her beautiful face when she tries to smile.

I shrug my shoulders uncertain what to say and try to find comforting words. 'How awful,' I say. 'Poor Audrey was certainly a dreadful sight and something that's hard to get out of your mind - hopefully, the image will lessen with time for you all.'

'I'm hoping so but am worried that seeing Audrey dead has traumatised them,' she says and sighs. 'They seemed okay when we got back yesterday and ate supper then went to bed but we've all been awake through the night. So, I don't know whether to take them home to Mum because she always knows what to do.'

Well, I think scathingly, most mothers do unless they were like mine, an alcoholic who never knew what time of day it was. My mum was totally useless. Some people who have had troubled childhoods complain they were left alone but I could never say that. Much to my chagrin, I'd wished my parents had gone out more often to leave me alone. Instead, they never left their stash of booze and drugs in the house, unless it was to collect the benefit and more supplies.

As opposed to this, I think of Barbie's Mam who is a tower of strength even in her eighties. When I'd first met Barbie, I had been envious that she was surrounded by people who loved and cared about her. However, this envy soon changed because they began to shower me with the same affection. Now, I love spending time with them all and enjoy nothing more than being in her mam's house when it's full of friends and relatives, especially at Christmastime. Barbie's Mam has had what I would call a rich life, has vast experience and knowledge about most matters. I know she would be well placed to advise Amber. However, I don't mention my own shambolic mother because it would only sound bitter.

I know that Amber doesn't need harsh comments at the moment and swallow hard then say, 'Ah, Mum's usually know what to do for the best, don't they?'

Amber nods. 'I figure I should too, but I don't,' she says. 'So, I'm going to ring her now and see what she thinks.'

'Great idea and let me know if there's anything I can do to help.'

She smiles fully for the first time and her eyes lighten. 'Thanks, Clive, but my partner, Kieran is finishing work a day early and arriving tomorrow,' she says. 'So, if the girls settle down more when he's here I'll decide then what to do.'

I wish her well and turn the corner to my caravan wondering how she can have a partner and still act in a provocative manner with other men. Or maybe it's just me who she gives the glad eye to? I can't understand this and sigh.

What if I'd been a chancer two nights ago and had accepted the offer of pizza, wine, and a little bit of fun. What would have happened? Would I have been kicked out of the caravan for Kieran? And what if he'd found out about the bit of fun? Sweat forms on my forehead. Lucky escape, me thinks. Arriving at the door to my caravan, I decide Barbie is right, when it comes to women, I haven't got a clue. Shrugging my shoulders, I open the door deciding relationships are a law unto themselves.

***

I settle down with my laptop but stay inside the caravan. I know if I go out onto the veranda there's a chance of meeting more neighbours and for the moment I just want to be on my own.

I think of how it's such an easy action to turn the knob and open a caravan or lodge door. Well for all of us it is, but would it be the same for Audrey in a confused state? Did she put the light on in the hall or open the door in the dark? Of course, she knew their lodge like the back of her hand – they've lived there for so long. However, why would she go outside that night when she never had done before? Did she see something outside through the window? Was someone in the garden? What was it that made Audrey search on her own rather than call for Liz?

Last year when I was involved in crime situations in York, I had managed to solve the issues by thinking of people and their state of minds. Barbie had teased and called me a super sleuth, but I wasn't. We'd had a day trip to Harrogate scouring second-hand shops for a stolen painting and in one of the shops, there'd been a battered old briefcase of soft leather and a felt, trilby-shaped hat. She'd bought them for me, and I'd worn the hat all day in the rain. Now, I wouldn't be without my briefcase – it goes everywhere with me especially to my writing group.

I smile knowing they're at home waiting for me and think again about Audrey's personality and, why she had gone outside. I'm used to creating characters in my novels where I get inside a person's mind. This way I can figure out how they think and get to know them better even though they're figments of my imagination. The man who mugged me had been desperate to save his restaurant and family from ruin which had nearly tipped him over the edge and into being a thief. The young gang of pick-pocketers had been at risk of being evicted from a hostel which would have sent them back out onto the streets to live. There's always a reason for people's action.

I sigh, but what was Audrey's reason? And how do I second guess someone's mind that is deranged and confused. Liz had said she was having a good day and had been quite lucid at bedtime. But had she still been coherent during the night when she went out through the back door? I shrug. I don't know enough about Alzheimer's to make this decision. However, something or somebody had to be involved with Audrey's demise.

I Google the definition of Alzheimer's. It tells me, Alzheimer's is a progressive neurologic disorder that causes the brain and its cells to shrink. It is the most common cause of dementia. There is a continuous decline in thinking, behavioural and social skills that affects a person's ability to function independently.

I nod and think of Jim. So, if it's the commonest cause then it's a knocking bet that he will either have it now or be getting it sooner rather than later. I also learn there is increased memory loss, an inability to learn new things, difficulty with language and problems when reading and writing, an inability to organise thoughts and think logically with a shortened attention span. People with this disease struggle to cope with new situations.

I feel incredibly sorry for people who are suffering in this way and cannot imagine as an author the inability to write and collect my thoughts in some type of order. It's what I've always done. I frown at the thought of not forming sentences and misuse of correct words to express what I'm trying to say.

I read on about Terry Pratchett and Iris Murdock then shake my head – it must have been torture for them. They were both in their early sixties when symptoms appeared of dementia. I gasp at this because sixty is not classed as being old nowadays. When I was younger, sixty seemed to be old, but now I'm in my thirties and it's not that far away, I shudder.

The stats from the Alzheimer's Association are chilling. It tells me there are over 42,000 people in the country aged sixty living with this condition. I'm shocked at these figures and quiver with dread.

Of course, people are living longer now, therefore, Audrey starting with memory loss at the age of eighty-five is acceptable. At her funeral, people will use the saying, she's had a good innings, but I think of my neighbour at home who at sixty-three, has just run a marathon and last year did a bungy-jump. He keeps telling me, 'I've still got a lot of living to do.'

I ease back on my seat and ponder. Men in their sixties are still having kids or have teenage children and do a good job of raising and organising their children's lives. Therefore, early dementia for these men must be horrendous if they're aware that in a few years' time they might not even recognise their own family.

I continue to read about Terry's dementia and how it started at the back of his brain when he struggled to see things properly. The shapes of the letters and words seemed to be jumbled up and didn't mean anything. It's hard to understand how dire this must have been for Terry when he was writing. It was his life and meant everything to him. Which is how it is for me now. My two part time jobs which fill my working days hold little interest to me at all – they're simply a source of income.

I look at the last sentence I've just written and rub my jaw trying to imagine the words all mixed-up. I shudder and feel scared which I figure is how people must be at the onset of symptoms. And, although Jim's manner was brusque and harsh when he talked about Audrey, I now understand how frightened he must feel.

I drain the warmish coffee from my mug. As a test, I write a jumble of words that are purposely mixed up. Shone the day bright - instead of - the day shone bright. Did Terry and Iris not realise these words were jumbled when they saw them on the screen, or did they know but just couldn't put them right?

I try to shake the miserable thoughts from my mind by looking at the small photograph I brought and placed on the unit. It is Barbie and I outside York Minster huddled together in the wind but laughing into the camera lens.

I smile. She would tell me just to be thankful that it hasn't happened and to get on with things. Thinking of her fills me with positive thoughts and I force myself back into my novel with the character, Jason Jennings, my young detective.

He's eagerly on the trail to catching the murderer in Durham and although he is a figment of my imagination, I can't help thinking about the difference between him and Ted Barker the DI we met yesterday.

I write, 'Jason crouched underneath the window pane outside the man's house. He was certain it had been him that murdered the young student in her accommodation. Jason always worked on his instinct and knew somewhere deep down in his gut that he was the one. This was the man who had slashed and strangled the girl. His heckles rose. No matter how long it took for the man to return home, he would wait. Jason grinned, he would arrest him today if it was the last thing he did!'

I sip my coffee and groan at the interruption when my mobile rings. I'd just gotten into my stride again but answer the call with a cheery, 'Hello.'

'Hi, Clive, it's me, Liz. I've just had a call to say the Inspector is on his way to talk to me,' she says. 'I don't suppose you could come around?'

Chapter Seventeen

I've pulled on my flying jacket and ran around to Liz in her lodge. I sigh hurrying through the gate in the picket fence knowing already I have thought of the lodge belonging to Liz without Audrey.

Liz is waiting for me at the door, and I step inside.

'Thanks for coming,' she says. 'I hope I'm not stopping you from writing and getting your book finished?'

I'm amazed at her forethought when she's in such an upset state. 'Nooo, not at all – let me worry about that - it's fine.'

Walking down the hall and into the lounge I'm already impressed with the size. It's almost as big as some bungalows or ground floor flats I've seen. The lounge is a good square shaped room with a cream leather sofa and two big chairs on either side of an electric fire in a marble fireplace. Although Celia is proud of her caravan and it's high-class it does have a look of transiency, but this lodge is more of a home. It's obvious they've not spared a penny in the décor and soft-furnishings – it's classy and very comfortable.

I look at the choice of two chairs and notice one is a rocker type with an old-fashioned knitted cushion. I could be wrong, but I figure this might have been Audrey's chair, so I plop down into the opposite one just in case this is upsetting for Liz.

I think she notices and appreciates my consideration because she smiles and nods.

'It's going to take a while for me to stop seeing Mam rocking in that chair,' she mutters.

I nod. 'It's bound to, Liz,' I say. 'Take it one day at a time.'

She looks better this morning. I can tell she's at least showered, washed her hair and changed her clothes. However, she still has no makeup on her face and her eyes are puffed and red rimmed. It looks like she's cried all night which is understandable. She offers me a coffee, but I refuse.

'I've just had one,' I say. 'But you get yourself one or I could make it for you?'

She shakes her head. 'Aww, that's kind of you but I'm floating in cups of tea at the moment. Two of my friends have called already and another of the older cleaners which is kind of them.'

I smile. 'And did the cleaner stay with you last night?'

She tuts. 'No, I wouldn't let her. I just wanted to be on my own. My aunt is travelling up from Devon today and will be staying until the funeral at least.'

'Well, that's good,' I say, but see her frown. 'Or maybe not so good?'

'Oh, she's alright I suppose but I've never got along with her much. Even though she's Mam's sister they're like chalk and cheese,' Liz says. 'If you think of Mary Poppins flying in clicking her heels and shouting, spit-spot, that'll be her.'

I chuckle and then feel my cheeks flush about joking at such a sad time. 'Sorry,' I mumble.

'Hey, don't be, if Mam was here, she'd laugh herself because that's what she called her, but I think, especially in their younger days they'd been very close.'

I look over into the corner of the room and see a highly polished bookcase with four shelves of novels in old covers. My natural curiosity gets the better of me and I ask, 'May I?'

Liz smiles. 'Oh, yeah, you being an author will be interested in those books.'

I hurry across and realise the novels are Agatha Christie works. It looks to be all sixty six of her books and the short story collections. I trace my fingers across the covers. They are all here, The Murder of Rodger Ackroyd, The Mysterious Affair at Styles, and I whistle through my teeth, at my firm favourite, And Then There Were None. I pick it out and open the front cover. Of course, they're not first editions but all the novels have their original covers from when they were bought.

Liz says, 'Both Mam and Aunt Maud were great readers and when she first moved down to Devon as a young woman, she posted Agatha Christie books up for Mam. They were usually for her birthday and Christmas presents. But I think they're all there.'

I nod. 'They sure are - it's an amazing collection,' I say and turn to her with the book in my hand. 'The old covers are fantastic – thanks for letting me see these.'

Liz sighs. 'I feel like I've given you the wrong impression of Maud because amongst her flaws, she is really very kind,' she says. 'On one of our visits to Tiverton where she lives, we went to Torquay for the weekend. She took us to the Agatha Christie Museum and then onto the sea tractor over to Burgh Island. We had lunch at The Pilchard Inn because we couldn't afford the posh hotel, but Mam and I loved seeing it all. In fact,' she continues with tears in her eyes, 'Mam talked about it for weeks when we got home, and Hercules's little grey cells was something we laughed about every time we watched David Suchet in the TV show.'

I smile and return the novel to its rightful place noticing they are in order of the year they were written. 'Oh, great. Burgh Island is on my bucket list of places to visit,' I say just as there's a tap at the front door.

Liz jumps up and hurries along the hall. I wander over to the large front window and look out. Ted is on his own at the door step but there are two police cars at reception. I watch the same policewoman as yesterday and another two officers split up and head along the three main walkways between the caravans. I presume they'll be talking to holidaymakers about Audrey. I figure because they've already done this once something must have shown up on the coroner's preliminary report.

Ted strides into the room followed quickly by Liz. He refuses tea and perches on the end of the sofa. I can see Liz is flustered when she sits down in her chair, but I remain standing with my hands in the side pockets of my jacket. There's an air of tension between the three of us and Liz wrings her hands as though she is bracing herself for what's to come.

Ted nods at me and wipes his hand across his forehead. I can tell he's sweating when he slips his anorak back from his shoulders. He's used the trick of not ironing the body of his white shirt and only the sleeves. Hmmm, I think, and Barbie reckons I'm lazy. I reckon it gives a sloppy impression, but I clear my mind and pay attention.

'So, Ms Mathews,' he says. 'Of course, we'll have to wait until the post mortem report to ascertain the exact cause of death, but what we can say now is that Mrs Mathews didn't die on those steps she was placed there.'

I gasp and Liz groans loudly. She puts a hand over her mouth and begins to rock backwards and forwards. I hurry over to her, sit on the arm of the chair and put my hand on her shoulder. I can feel her body trembling and I try to mumble reassurances.

Ted sighs. 'I know it's an awful shock so in the meantime the pathologist has classed this as a suspicious death,' he says. 'He can't say for sure but thinks Mrs Mathews was already dead when she went into the sea. There are markings on the top step which show that she was dragged there and in the grassy verge to the side are big footprints.'

This guy reminds me of Jack Frost on TV in his later days although I think the actor, David Jason showed much more humanity and empathy to the victims' relatives. I decide Ted could definitely do with learning a bedside manner as they say in hospitals. He looks tired and weary as if it's an effort to talk to us.

Liz leans into me and I wrap my arm around her. Once again, she sobs into my shoulder.

I ask, 'Okay, and have you any idea of what time this occurred?'

Ted nods. 'Yes, around the footprints the grass was dry therefore we reckon she had to be put there when the tide was out, or his shoes would have been wet. And they weren't,' he says. 'The pathologist has put the time of death between 11pm and 4am which fits in with the timing of the tides that night. Of course, this will be clarified at the post mortem but we will need you to identify Mrs Mathews.'

I look at Ted's face which is expressionless. His cheeks are rosy-red, and his thin lips are forced into a tight half-smile. Yep, I think, there's no energy or drive left in this man at all – he's obviously paying us lip service.

'Right, thanks,' I say and turn to look at Liz. 'Can I make you a cup of tea?'

At the sound of my voice, she grabs a tissue and wipes her wet face. She shakes her head. 'I…I can't believe this is happening.'

Ted sits forward with his hands clasped between his knees. 'And you never heard her get up through the night or know what time she left?'

What an idiotic question, I think and take in a deep breath. As I'm contemplating a sarcastic remark, I see Liz pull back her shoulders.

She tuts and picks up her packet of cigarettes from the coffee table. 'Look, how many times do I have to say this? I went to bed at 11.30 and no, I never heard a thing all night. I've told your policewoman this at least five times,' she shouts. 'Do you guys not talk to each other? And, do any of you know what Alzheimer's actually is?'

I can't help smiling to myself at her straightforward manner and tone. It's exactly what I was thinking but maybe wouldn't have had the nerve to say. In any other situation I would have given her a round of applause, but I stay silent letting her take the lead.

Ted sits back and pushes his arms through the sleeves of his anorak again. 'It's understandable that you're upset, Ms Mathews,' he says. 'So, I'll leave you to it and return when I've more news.'

He gets up and I gesture for Liz to stay seated while I follow Ted to the hall to see him out.

As a parting shot, he turns and says over his shoulder, 'You know, to solve a crime you have to look at it a little differently and sometimes the simplest solution turns out to be the right one.'

Ted stomps back out the front door and I sigh. And that's supposed to mean what exactly? Is he annoyed that the findings are suspicious? Would it have made his life easier if the result had been that a dotty old lady wandered down the steps, fell in the sea and drowned?

I head back into the lounge knowing if that was the case then this would have been neatly tied up in a few days whereas now he's got something much harder and more tangled to deal with. I get the feeling that Audrey's case is simply a nuisance to him.

Liz has lit up a cigarette and is puffing smoke out into the lounge. We talk through everything Ted has told her. When her mobile rings I head out of the back door promising to ring later.

***

Heading back to my caravan I can't help feeling justified. I'd known from the start of this that there was something other than a lost old lady. And now it's a suspicious death.

Later that night, I talk to Barbie on her mobile and explain what's happened. 'I really hope they do a proper investigation because if they don't and the murderer gets to walk away scot-free then he might kill another old lady on the coast.'

Barbie agrees and I continue, 'Although I reckon this is not a random assault and murder. Audrey couldn't have been robbed for money because in a nightdress she wasn't carrying any,'

I say. 'So, she has to have been targeted by someone who knew and wanted to harm her.'

Barbie answers, 'Or perhaps she got into an altercation with a gang of thugs that went sadly wrong.'

Chapter Eighteen

Liz

Yesterday, when they'd found her mam in the sea, Liz felt it had been some type of punishment. She knew her thoughts were erratic because of the shock, but every time Liz thought of her lying in the freezing water all on her own, she got pains in her chest and her stomach lurched. It was as though Mam was chastising her for not being there. Liz didn't think she'd ever get over the feelings of guilt. Her lovely Mam had died alone.

Liz had choked back sobs praying Mam hadn't been too scared. In fact, she prayed that Audrey had been completely fogged over when she'd left the lodge and wouldn't have known anything about what happened and hadn't suffered. If Mam had been relatively lucid – she would have been terrified. This thought made Liz's stomach churn until she'd felt bile rise in the back of her throat.

Over the years, Liz had often imagined the day when Audrey would pass over and the circumstances. She'd anticipated being there holding her hand and kissing her forehead when Mam took her last breaths. All she'd ever wanted was for her death to be peaceful and painless, but the horrible appearance of her bloated face in the sea had made Liz groan out loud. Liz knew she would never rid herself of this image.

They'd had discussions on her lucid days and talked about her funeral in the cemetery, in fact Audrey had bought the plot years ago. And Liz had promised that she would be by her side whether it was in hospital or in the lodge. Liz sobbed knowing she hadn't kept this promise.

The day Audrey was diagnosed, she'd said to Liz, 'I'd rather die than live with Alzheimer's!'

However, in the last few years Mam hadn't been coherent enough to have such logical thoughts. Liz sighed, half the time she didn't know the difference between Rice Krispies and Cornflakes.

When the cleaner had left the night before she'd pulled back her shoulders, lit a cigarette, and rang her Aunt Maud. It hadn't been an easy conversation because she'd never really liked her and the words, your sister has died, seemed to stick in her throat. Liz had sobbed out the last few sentences about what had happened and her unexplained death.

Maud had been sharp with her. 'Elizabeth, get a hold of yourself,' she'd snapped. Liz had pulled a face at her mobile and ended the conversation. Much like she had done as a teenager.

Maybe, it was because Maud always called her, Elizabeth when no one else ever had done even though it was the name on her birth certificate. Mam had called her, Lizzie, for as long as she could remember.

She'd flung herself onto Audrey's bed and lain there struggling to believe that she had actually gone. The silence in the lodge had seemed deafening. Not that they'd been noisy together, but the TV was always turned up so Audrey could hear the voices. For years, they had pottered around the rooms together from the bedrooms to the lounge to the kitchen.

Audrey had taken to following Liz around and standing behind at her shoulder. Mam had often said, 'I feel safer if I can see you.'

Being at her shoulder had grated on Liz after a while, but now she longed to hear her trailing slippers going from room to room. She pined to hear the plodding on the carpets and the vinyl in the kitchen. It dawned upon her that she'd never hear Mam call her name again. She'd never hear her shaky voice shouting, 'Lizzie, are you there? Where are you?'

Liz cried long into the night. After all the years she'd looked after Audrey and kept her safe she had died an awful death and Liz hadn't been there to protect her. 'I've let her down very badly,' she howled into the empty room.

Ruffling up the pillows behind her head Liz had sobbed into the top one. She'd been sure Audrey's smell still lingered on the bedlinen but knew that was irrational. Mam's smell had been a sweet, face-powdery aroma that clung around her head and neck. Liz had smelt it all her life especially when she was little and hugged her tight.

The pillowcase had been wet with tears, so she'd flipped it over and pushed her face back into the softness. Suddenly she had felt something hard inside.

Liz had sworn, 'WTF!'

She'd pushed her hand inside the pillowslip and pulled out an old card. It was a black & white photograph of a young soldier in uniform, and she had known it was very old. Liz knew in those days photography was in its infancy and images were often developed onto cards. There were a few like this of her grandparents in Mam's old photo album. Liz frowned - she'd never seen this image before. Who was he? And if the soldier was important, why wasn't he in the album?

Since Audrey's confusion started, they'd regularly looked through the family shots and her mam would name them all. Liz had written under each photo who they were and the date to jog her memory.

Liz had shuffled off the bed with the card in her hand and hurried into the lounge. She'd spread the album open on top of the coffee table and systematically went through page after page looking for a resemblance to this soldier. A second cousin? A family friend? But there'd been nothing. Audrey had very old photos of her mother and father on their wedding day, but they'd died when she was only fourteen in a tram accident in Blackpool. Audrey often told

her that Maud had raised her, and Liz nodded –
that was why they'd been so close.

Liz looked closer at two photos of Aunty Maud
and her daughter, Sheila. She was her only
cousin and worked in Africa at the moment. She
looked from their faces to the soldier's face but
there'd been no resemblance.

Over the years they'd visited Maud a couple of
times, but as the two sisters had gotten older the
visits declined. Liz reckoned it had to be over
five years since they'd taken the train down to
see Maud. It had been just after Audrey was
diagnosed with Alzheimer's when her lucid days
far outnumbered her confused days.

Maud had flown up to them two years ago for
Christmas. She'd been most upset when Audrey
hadn't known who she was and couldn't
associate the regular Sunday morning phone
calls with the woman sitting on the sofa. Maud
was the elder sister by eighteen months, but
unlike Audrey, her memory was still as clear as
it had always been.

Liz had sighed and looked at the photograph
again wondering if the soldier had been
anything to do with her? Mam had told her that
Liz's father was her first relationship with a
man. And, of course, in the album there was a
photograph of Audrey with her father, Duncan.
She scrutinised their faces and compared their
features to the soldiers, but nothing – still no
resemblance.

So, she'd frowned, who the hell was he? And why was this card hidden in her pillowcase? Liz knew it was the gesture of a woman who wanted the photograph kept safe. Had he been an old boyfriend after Duncan left? Or a friend who Audrey had hoped would become something more.

Liz knew that if the photo was in her bed, Mam must have looked at it often and also that she'd hidden it every fortnight when the cleaners stripped her bed linen. Liz had flown back into Mam's bedroom and went through her bedside cabinets, dressing table and drawers, trinket boxes, and jewellery box but there was nothing else. She had finally dozed off into a troubled sleep for a few hours before daybreak, showered and dressed knowing the police would return.

When they did, she planned to ring Clive because he had offered to be with her during their visit. It was strange, Liz mused, how on the morning Clive arrived she'd had flirtatious notions about him.

He had been a complete stranger but during the last two days she had become reliant upon him. Clive had been there for her when there'd been no one else. He had supported her through all the stress and worry when Mam was missing. And yesterday when they'd found her body, Liz knew she would have been lost without him. He was kind, reassuring, and seemed to know exactly when she needed to talk, and indeed when she didn't. Once again, Liz thought what a lucky woman his fiancé was.

Liz had taken a deep breath knowing there was bound to be more news today and felt the tears flow once more. No matter what they told her, Audrey would still be dead and nothing on God's earth was ever going to bring her back.

***

Now that Clive and the inspector have gone Liz tries to fill in the time until Aunt Maud arrives. She is flying up to Newcastle airport and taking a taxi from there. She has refused help of any kind saying that she would rather make her own way. Liz knew this is just how Maud does things and sighs. It isn't going to be an easy time having her stay, but Liz knows asking her to go into a hotel isn't an option. First, she is an old lady who needs her creature comforts and second, she is after all, Mam's family.

Liz arranges for the staff to give the lodge a thorough clean so Maud can't criticise if everything isn't ship-shape. It's going to be bad enough having her sleep in Mam's bedroom, she thinks, but knows Audrey would want it this way.

The only highlight of today, is that Maud might know who this soldier is? Standing in the garden smoking a cigarette she decides that for once in her life, she's longing for Maud to arrive. Liz looks up to see a taxi outside heralding her arrival, she stubs out her cigarette, and hurries to greet her.

Chapter Nineteen

The next morning, I set off to visit Seaton Delaval Hall. With Audrey's unexplained death spinning around in my mind I can't focus to write. The weather is alternating between sea-fret and drizzle, so the veranda is wet and there's no view across the sea to the lighthouse.

Feeble excuse I can hear my fellow author friends cry. It's going to be hard to write when I get back home into my little office staring out over the back garden. Which as hard as we try usually resembles a jungle. Neither of us could call ourselves gardeners although Barbie seems to enjoy it more than I do. And, although I call it my office it's actually just the second bedroom which I converted into a place to write when my ex-wife left.

It's damp and humid as I walk, so I pull off my jacket and fling it over my shoulder. In the short distance from my caravan to the roadside, I pass at least three sets of people and am surprised to see how everyone speaks. It's only small snippets like, 'morning' or 'shame the weather's changed' or 'we'll not be on the beach today' but, I decide, it is a friendly place to stay on holiday.

I reckon it's almost like a happy camping community but with no tents only caravans. Maybe it's the fresh air and walking on the grass in between the caravans that makes everyone want to be pleasant. Not that the caravans are cramped together because there's a good amount of space amongst the rows. I smell wafts of cooked breakfasts, and everyone seems to have dogs to walk. I suppose it's a good place to be with animals rather than holidaying in hotels which are not dog friendly.

It's very different to being at home in city surroundings where everyone is cooped up in their gardens and houses. Although, I must admit in our area of York we do have good people living in the terrace and a strong Neighbourhood Watch. Still, I don't speak to as many people as this when I walk down the streets to work every morning.

I leave through the main entrance and instead of turning left down to the seafront I turn right and cross over the road to the bus stop. I don't wait long, flag down the 308 bus and sit in the front seat. The driver has told me he'll shout when we get to the stop for Seaton Delaval Hall.

***

I hop down from the bus and look at the spectacular sight in front of me. There's a wide expanse of grass in front of the hall which, in all its glory, is massive. I wander up the drive nearing a big statue in front of the lower middle section of the hall. It is David holding his empty sling and looking down at Goliath. There are two higher wings to the east and west. The sun is shining on all the old stone, and I gasp in awe – it's stunningly beautiful.

The information pamphlet I'd picked up from Liz in reception tells me that the hall was built

by Sir John Vanburgh. He was also known for
building Blenheim Palace and Castle Howard in
Yorkshire. I'm amazed to see this is only fifteen
miles from York although I 've never been to the
castle. Note to myself, Barbie and I must go to
visit one day. If it's anything like this amazing
structure it will be worth seeing.

Captain Francis Delaval and his wife, Rhoda
were the first generation to move into the hall
with their twelve children. I smile thinking how
there would have been plenty of room for the
kids to run around in the extensive grounds -
they must have had a field day.

All the male and female members of the family
were models of grace and beauty. The men were
perfect Adonises. I chuckle, a bit like myself, I
think pulling back my shoulders, or not, as the
case may be.

The pamphlet tells me how they lived for
enjoyment and love. The family were gay and
wild, and Lord Delaval entertained an almost
continuous crowd of company. The frequent
fêtes and masquerades that were given converted
the house and gardens into a fairyland with
throngs of people frolicking around.

I begin to follow the path around to the car park
and entrance deciding this isn't a bad motto to
have in life – enjoyment and fun.

I enter the ticket office, pay £10 entrance fee
and with another map of the hall I slowly walk
towards the back entrance. After extensive
renovations on the balcony, it is open alongside

the east wing, collection store, salon, and basement.

I read how the family played unusual pranks on their guests, much to their amusement, but not the actual victims. The house was fitted with strange devices to perform these practical jokes. Beds were suspended by pulleys over trapdoors, so that when the guests had retired and were falling asleep, they would be ditched into a cold bath.

Another gadget used partitions between sleeping rooms which could be suddenly hoisted up into the ceiling. This meant that when ladies and gentlemen were in various stages of undress the walls of the rooms would disappear in a moment and guests would find themselves in a gathering of mixed sexes and in an embarrassing plight.

Francis Blake Delaval II had a particularly fun time living here as a child. He often played practical jokes on visitors, who risked waking up in a room arranged upside down, so they appeared to be sleeping on the ceiling. I can't help laughing at this and know Barbie's niece and nephew would find this hilarious fun.

I stop at a flat weighing scale in the gravel path with a small information board. It tells me that Lord Delaval wanted to copy the King who had a scale in Sandringham which weighed guests before and after they had been to stay. Apparently, it was their way of determining if the guests had enjoyed the food. I shake my head and figure now is not a good time to see if the scales are correct because I've been eating more than usual in the caravan.

The extensive grounds lie to my left and there is a big wooden box of children's field games. I watch grandparents with two children playing cricket with a bat and ball. This makes me smile because I can see they're loving the visit.

When I walk through the basement there's a musky aroma and in some places, it almost smells damp. It's dark and dingy but my eyes quickly adjust from the light outside. Noises of old ships mooring, and aged timber creaking fill the first room to create an eerie atmosphere with a huge, and I mean, huge anchor – it fills the entire space. I whistle through my teeth in wonder and take more photographs. I love the connection of the family, to St. Mary's lighthouse, and the sea which plays an integral part in Whitley Bay's heritage.

I read how in January 1822, sailors off Whitley Bay coast noticed that the sunset seemed unnaturally brilliant and then realised the hall was on fire. I wonder if they'd used the monks lantern on the tower to keep them well away from the dangerous rocks around the island and causeway? At the thought of poor Audrey on those causeway steps, I shudder knowing it's going to take a while to rid myself of those images.

Thinking of how those sailors must have felt on ships with fathoms of water underneath them but were so far away they couldn't even dampen the flames. The central hall was gutted and has remained an empty shell ever since.

Turning up a few steps onto a long corridor with a plush red carpet runner down the middle I decide it helps to detract my eye from the old stone walls. While walking, I count ten big round windows in the left hand side of the corridor which all overlook the garden. The last window has a red-rose bush planted outside which looks picture perfect, clever gardener, I reckon and smile.

Of course, the hall would have been here when Audrey decided to open the caravan park and I nod in respect to her commercial entrepreneurship. It's in a great position and must have been advantageous for both of them with tourism.

At the end of the corridor are portraits of the Delaval family. I stop to gaze at George who commissioned the build of the hall. In his classy, velvet long-jacket and gold buttons he looks wealthy and majestic. He's wearing a long blonde wig which has thick curls. God, I reckon. it must have been very hot to walk around wearing that in the summer. However, when I look closer at the portrait, I can see that along with his rosy red cheeks, he has a pleasant face and kind eyes.

A further portrait catches my eye and I literally feel my mouth drop open. It's a painting of Lady Hastings who was the last occupant in the hall before it was sold to The National Trust. Apart from Barbie, there's not many women who I think look more lovely, but this lady makes me stop dead in my tracks – she is absolutely stunning. Or could it be the talented artist who painted her?

Lady Hasting's skin is almost translucent, and her blonde wavy hair is piled high. It looks soft and curvy, as is her figure with a low-cut pastel dress. A big pearl necklace draws the eye down to her cleavage but only in a subtle way. And tiny pearl ear rings glistened at her ears. Her thin delicate eyebrows frame big eyes as she wears a smug expression, but in an understated manner. She's not brash and showing off just slightly superior which I suppose she was in her hey-day.

This would make a great short story, I reckon and along with an abundance of other ideas I head for a coffee. The brewhouse café is what used to be the coach house and I amble inside for cheesecake and coffee. It's a light airy room and I sit down at one of the wooden tables. I think of the huge anchor and the sailors gathered on deck of their ship looking across to the hall on fire and scribble down a conversation between two of the sailors. I know I can weave this into a story later.

Sipping the hot coffee, I recall Lady Hastings and know her husband must have worshipped this beautiful lady, much as I do, Barbie. I scribble down a love story between them and smile to myself. More plots for shorter stories fly through my mind including the old hall and French ancestry. I smile knowing I'll be able to use the information sheets I have gathered. Making copious notes I check the photographs of paintings and gardens that I've taken.

I'm transfixed with all the history especially about the Second World War and how German prisoners also worked in the nearby farms. They lived in the East Wing of the hall in the rabbit-warren corridors. On the wall is a fire extinguisher with instructions in both English and German. There are still drawings of the games the POWs played as a past time. The wing apparently was commissioned by the War Office between 1939 and 1948. It is said that some of the prisoners voluntarily stayed on after the war ended.

Leaving the hall, I decide the visit has been worthwhile because it's filled my mind with different thoughts other than my novel. When I'm writing a book, I tend to get so caught up with my characters and storyline that I border on obsessional so learning about the hall has been a refreshing change and I head back to the caravan park.

Chapter Twenty

Finally, I've had a great night's sleep so am feeling refreshed and revived. I heap cereal into a bowl, splash them with cold milk and crunch to my heart's content watching the news on TV.

I remember my telephone conversation with Barbie and how she advised me not to get too caught up in the issue of Audrey's unexplained death. And I know she's right. However, because I've had a certain amount of involvement already with Liz, I feel that it's beyond me to switch off and walk away completely. Anyway, the mystery of what's happened tugs in my gut.

I suppose it's a little like the whodunit part of my writing. I have to know what's happened and why. Although my brain is fired up with the unknown, I sigh knowing it doesn't feel right to be comparing the death of a much loved old lady with writing imaginary fiction. I grimace, it may seem callous to other people, but it's who I am, an author, and who I've been for three years now.

I had started writing about six months before my ex-wife left and it had been one of her accusatory comments in the last argument we'd had. She ranted, 'You're always at that bloody desk or scribbling in a note book – all I ever see is the top of your head – you never even look up at me nowadays!'

And when she'd gone off with her basketball player, I had missed her of course, but had to admit I loved the freedom to please myself. When I met Barbie, it had been easier because she knew it's what I do. I write. And in the future, I'm hoping to be a successful full-time author who can make a reasonable living at something I do well.

It's my little daydream, imaging my books selling thousands of copies with a traditional publisher. Which in turn means I would be able to finish working in the travel agency and kiss goodbye to the York City Tours. Although, I grin, I do still enjoy being a tour leader mainly because I love our historic city of York.

So, with my head still in the clouds I step out of the caravan intending to walk along the seafront. The sky is overcast this morning but there's a promise of sunshine by midday which will be great timing to sit and write on the veranda. I pull up the collar of my jacket and lock the caravan then set off.

When I saunter along the lodge path, I smile to see an old, white-haired lady in the kitchen window washing dishes. Ah, I think, Aunt Maud has arrived and true to Liz's description of Mary Poppins, she's obviously working her magic in the kitchen.

I'd seen the film years ago when I was twelve on a school trip and grin at the memories. It was my first trip to the cinema in Doncaster and although I had been with my schoolmates, and it hadn't been deemed a cool thing, secretly I loved Mary Poppins. The bright colours, costumes, dancing and singing were like a glowing light in my drab existence at home. It, or should I say, Mary Poppins, gave me hope that there were better things to come. There was fun, laughter, and gaiety in life with nice people around if I looked hard enough to find it all.

I lengthen my stride now and head down to the seafront continuing along past the Spanish City determined to explore what lies further along the coastline. It's early so there aren't many people around except for a few solitary dog walkers. The sea is calm with thick clouds hanging over the little ripples on the shore. Not the right time to paddle today, I reckon, but know by this afternoon when the sun comes out so will all the holidaymakers.

Rounding the bend of the coastline I walk into Cullercoats with its semi-circular sandy beach. It's a small town in-between Whitley Bay and Tynemouth and I read on a plaque that the harbour is the home of The Dove Marine Laboratory within Newcastle University.

After a disaster out at sea, the Duke of Northumberland funded the setting up of the RNLI lifeboat station. The Brigade House and watchtower were built and remained in use gaining seven gallantry awards until 2004 when a new station was built.

I stand in awe of the lifeboat house on the beach with its big red doors that open when needed to bring out the lifeboat. I read all about the service the lifeboat crew have given to the community and travellers out at sea and then whistle through my teeth in admiration. These were, and still are brave men and women who risk their lives every time they head out in the lifeboat.

I sit on a small bench looking down on the station and gaze out to sea. My mind is transported back to Durham and my novel. I try to think of a way to write my next chapter when Jason Jennings arrests a suspect for the student's murder.

Pulling out the small notebook from my jacket I write, 'Has to be an explosive scene. Keep sentences short. Readers don't want overly descriptive terms when there's lots of action. Must be fast paced. Jason has to get his man. The suspect is a big man with a history of violent assault. Therefore, Jason could, rightly so, feel intimidated, but my Detective Sergeant has youth, agility, and surprise on his side.'

I grin in satisfaction knowing I'm on the right track with Jason. He'll be like the Canadian Mounted Police, who always get their man. In fact, he is, and will continue to be, the exact opposite of Ted Barker. Deep in thought, I walk a little further around the coastline.

Inevitably, I head back the way I've come and into Whitley Bay town centre. Instead of hugging the shoreline I walk up onto the streets.

My mobile tingles with a text and I read a message from Liz. 'The blonde policewoman is taking me and Aunt Maud to identify Mam.'

I frown knowing this is going to be tough for them both and reply, 'Okay, take a deep breath - you know where I am if I can do anything to help.'

In the town centre I wander past the playhouse and look at the poster in the window advertising what is being shown. I wonder if I should treat Barbie and I to a play on our last night in the caravan. However, I shake my head deciding against this idea. I'm longing to have her near me and reckon we should just cosy-up in bed for the evening with a take away.

I continue along Park View remembering the TV program, Sunday Times Best Place To Live, and how Whitley Bay was voted number three. The cameras had been along this road looking at all of the speciality shops which I reckon do look cool and quirky. The presenter on the program told us how the community take great pride and are enthusiastic about their shops and high street. They've got this bang-on, I think, and rightly deserve the best place to live accolade.

I glance in the window of an amazing bookstore called, The Bound. I grin - what a fantastic name for a shop full of books. It has a classy frontage with two big windows either side of dark grey boarding with 'The Bound' in white lettering using a modern font. The windows hold two big cream boards with books on small holders. I sigh imagining my book being presented like this in a shop window for all the world, or the people of Whitley Bay, to see.

I know mine is displayed on reader's screens on Amazon and sigh, somehow, it's not the same. Although I'm a great advocate of eBooks and electronic devices, I still love to hold a paperback, or better still, a hardback book in my hands. I know I'm not alone in this theory because many readers do and wonder when the trend of electronic equipment loses its appeal, if we'll all revisit printed books like the return of vinyl records and players.

I wander inside the bookstore. It's equally impressive with white walls and white boarding. The boards have poems written on them and the white bookshelves are full of paper and hardback books.

A friendly looking guy behind the counter calls over to me, 'Hey there, just give me a shout if you need anything.'

I thank him and wander over to make conversation. His name badge tells me that he's the manager.

'It's a great bookstore you've got here,' I say.

He nods. 'Yeah, and we have another two branches, one in Corbridge and one in Alnwick.'

I'm impressed. Although I've never been to these places, I do know they're in Northumberland. I tell him about my first novel on Amazon and a little bit about myself. I bring up the Amazon page on my mobile with all the details of my first novel.

I'm truly amazed when he kindly offers to stock my book and class me as a Northern author. After some discussion we agree that he'll try a few copies initially, and we exchange business cards, and agree terms.

I can't help grinning. 'Hey, I guess this is my lucky day,' I say and shake his hand. 'Thanks so much for this – I'm thrilled at the opportunity.'

I leave the bookshop whistling with a spring in my step. The modern bookstores have had to re-vamp their image of late to compete with electronic devices and have gone a long way in pulling people back into traditional paperback and hardcopy reading. Many of the big bookstores like Waterstones now have coffee shops which create, not only more revenue, but a relaxed congenial atmosphere where readers can discuss all things bookish – it's my idea of heaven. I can't think of a single writer who doesn't love bookstores. It's a new route that I haven't ventured down as yet but decide that Amazon doesn't need to have the whole market to itself and grin.

I can tell in, The Bound, their passion for books is addictive. And I'm impressed that they've stayed viable during the difficult years of pandemic. Bookstores are socially part of our custom in the UK and essential to the areas they serve by connecting people with books to read. I wonder if I should approach our local bookstores in York? I'd somehow thought that the novel had to be set in the North to be considered by a

local author. But obviously not, if The Bound
are willing to take my London novel. And, I
think excitedly, if this sells reasonably well, my
Durham novel might be accepted too.

The cover of my book springs to mind and I
wonder what image to use to represent Durham
City. I wander up onto York Road and stop at
the tall glass windows of the library. I decide to
pop inside and see how other authors have
depicted Northern towns and cities.

Inside is as modern as the outside with bright
lime-green plastic chairs and tables. I saunter
past the main desk and smile at the woman who
greets me warmly. I begin by searching along
the bookshelves in the mysteries, thrillers, and
crime book section looking at covers. Of course,
there are many images of the iconic sights, Tyne
Bridge in Newcastle, The Angel of the North,
and Holy Island where L.J. Ross has some
amazing shots.

There's none I can see with Durham images
until I spot one from an author called, Helen
Cox. I haven't heard of this author, but the title,
Death Awaits in Durham, is printed over a side
view of the old cathedral and looks striking in
white letters. Hmmm, I think, food for thought,
and know I can ask Barbie for more ideas of
Durham views.

However, as my student is murdered in the
accommodation rooms at the old castle, I figure
an image of this would be appropriate. Many
authors think the cover should give some idea of

where the story is set or what the reader can expect, and subtitles often help with genre. I've already decided mine will read, Jason Jennings Investigates.

I turn slightly to face the back of the library and recognise a man sitting at a computer. I can't place his face at first, then recognition dawns. It's Dennis who stays in the caravan behind me at the park. I hesitate from approaching until I'm sure it's him but figure he's not hard to mistake being such a big man. I hover behind unsure of whether to greet him or not.

Libraries are strange places with traditional rules and regulations. I inhale the stuffy smell of oldish books and smile. They have a different atmosphere of hushed tones and whispering amongst readers who like their own space and quiet time. Unlike, The Bound, with its cheery, open conversational vibes. However, libraires do provide an invaluable free resource to the general public, especially for children. I remember hearing an American author speak at a festival who told us libraries don't exist in many parts of the USA and I'd been shocked.

Pretending to look at books on the shelf behind Dennis, I tussle with the idea of making conversation or not. My natural curiosity gets the better of me and I wonder what he's looking at on the computer. Dennis doesn't appear to see me because he's engrossed with information on the screen, so I creep up further to the side of him in front of the romantic novels section.

I note two elderly ladies looking at Mills and Boon books and grin. I know there's a market for all genre in books, but it is beyond me how these stereotypical romance stories interest readers.

Of course, I get it that these readers are almost, but not exclusively women, and I've said to Barbie in the past, 'What is it that's so awful in their lives that they constantly dream of escaping to different countries to meet wealthy millionaires. It's as though sun, sea, money, and love are the answer to all of their problems.'

Barbie had answered in her down to earth way. 'We all have dreams, Clive and you don't know what is in these women's lives. I think most people associate sun and beach holidays with relaxation and escapism.'

I smile knowing she is right and how I've viewed my caravan on the beach as somewhere to escape for peace and quiet to write. And, I also know that romantic fiction is a huge market making authors a small fortune in royalties. So, I conclude happily, there's nothing to say that women dreaming of millionaires are wrong and men like Jim who are hooked on crime thrillers are right. We are all different which is what makes people so very interesting.

I peer over Dennis's shoulder and am amazed at the size of his big jaw and jowls which wobble at the slightest movement in his face. His white false teeth seem too big for his small mouth, and I can see that he is grinding them by the clench of his jaw. I smile knowing that now his nickname will forever be, Slack-Jowls.

Looking further over his shoulder, I read the headline on the article he is scrolling through. It's about the history of Whitley Bay. And that is another avenue in a completely different genre of historical fiction. I turn slightly so I can see on the sidebar that his last log-in was about the history of Seaton Delaval Hall.

I nod to myself remembering my visit there and how absorbed I'd been in the history of the naughty pranksters who lived in the hall descended from France. I had thought it strange because I didn't think of the French as a race who enjoyed a joke and laughed a lot. Which, I sigh, is wrong of me to think this way because I've never set foot in their country.

Suddenly, I feel the presence of someone to my left and turn to see it is the librarian who was attending the desk and had greeted me warmly. She's very tall and is now wearing rimmed glasses which are perched on the end of her nose. Her tweed skirt, flat lace-ups and starched white shirt make me want to hoot. She looks like a typical old librarian who should work in The Bodleian Library in Oxford not in this lime green plastic environment.

I smile and nod at her, but she raises an eyebrow and folds her arms across her chest, as if to say, I've got my eye on you. Obviously, she isn't going to return my friendly greeting, and I scurry away towards the back door with her walking slowly behind me as though I'm being escorted from the premises.

Chapter Twenty One

I return to the caravan and sit on the veranda as the sun has finally arrived. I'd waved to Liz when passing the lodge as she was in the garden having a cigarette but didn't stop to talk. I figured she would need some time to herself after seeing Audrey.

Opening my laptop, I stare across at my usual view. The colours are spectacular, and I remember the painting in the Links Art Café. The pure white tower of the lighthouse against the bright blue sky is stunning. I wonder how it stays so white especially in the winter months. Perhaps they paint it regularly or maybe there's something in the salty sea air that helps keep it white.

My mobile is lying to my right hand side and it vibrates with Liz's name on the screen. I pick up straight away.

'I don't suppose you could pop over now?' Liz asks. 'The inspector is on his way and although Aunt Maud is here there might be something we don't understand.'

'Yeah, sure,' I say. 'It's not a problem.'

When I get there Liz is actually in reception. I see her through the window and wave – she beckons me inside.

Two of the younger receptionists are hovering behind Liz sitting at the desk. They are both dressed in blue flowered blouses with navy blue jackets and skirts. Although I've seen them from a distance over the last couple of days, I know their jobs are busy answering the telephones and making bookings. One of them shuffles her loafers on the cushion-flooring and I can tell the other girl looks equally apprehensive as she wrings her hands together. It's as though Liz is inspecting their work and there's a heavy silence between them.

Liz looks up at me and smiles. 'I thought I'd better keep a check on what's going on in the diary which seems crass at a time like this.'

I shake my head. 'I don't think so, from what you've told me Audrey would want you to keep on top of things – this caravan park was her life's work,' I say. 'But from what I can see the park is so well organised that it virtually runs itself.'

Liz nods and I watch her chew the inside of her cheek as though she's fighting back tears. Her head is down reading and then she looks up. 'It does but when we have a high turn-over of guests I like to keep a check on things,' she says. 'And it looks like there was a bit of a carry-on last night. The night-shift officer has left a note to say he'd had complaints about loud music playing at midnight up in dahlia section, so he called in the security company we use. They'd sent two men who asked the stag group to turn the music down which they did, and no further actions were needed.'

'Ah, right, I didn't know you had staff here during the night?' I say and make a mental note of this. I wonder if the police have questioned the night-shift officer to see if he saw anything of Audrey out in the garden that night. I figure they will have done, and watch Liz close the big diary.

'That's great, girls,' she says and wearily pushes her slight frame up from the chair. Their shoulders slump and they both whisper words of condolence to her.

Liz nods and looks at me. 'Come and meet, Aunt Maud,' she says.

I follow her out of the side door and walk around to their little path and the lodge.

Aunt Maud is the total opposite to what Audrey was. Once again, it's a surprise how quickly I'm thinking of the old lady in a past tense. Where Audrey was tall and thin with a regal stance about her, Maud is squat and round.

Maud shakes my hand as soon as we enter the hallway and I'm taken aback by her strong grip while she looks me up and down. At the age of nearly ninety two, I hope I have as much strength as this lady does and give her my best smile. I always think of this as my winning smile. When I had told Barbie this, she'd joked and said, 'You just look like a grinning idiot.'

Aunt Maud smiles back. 'I want to thank you for looking after Elizabeth in the last couple of days,' she says. 'My niece tells me that you've been a great help.'

Of course, Liz is a shortened version of Elizabeth. However, I'd never thought of Liz as such and don't think she suits her full name. I know names are often shortened to appear more approachable and friendlier which means they are warmer and less intimidating. Maybe it's because our queen was called, Elizabeth that I feel the name is formal and distant which Liz certainly isn't.

I nod my head. 'That's not a problem,' I say. 'I'm happy to help out at such a distressing time.'

I look at Maud who is staring intently at my face. My cheeks flush slightly under the close scrutiny. She abruptly turns and heads along to the lounge. I follow them both and notice that Audrey's bedroom door is ajar where I can see the neatly made bed.

I sigh knowing how difficult it must be for Liz to have Maud sleeping in her mam's bedroom. However, as there are only two bedrooms, I reckon she hasn't much choice in the matter.

Considering Maud's age, her skin is remarkably smooth, and her white hair is cut into a short pixie style framing her large eyes. She tells me about her flight up to Newcastle while Liz makes a pot of tea and carries the tray into the lounge.

Gone are the chunky Ikea mugs that Liz usually has, and I watch Maud automatically pour milk into our three china cups. The expression, shall I be mother, springs to my mind and I heap a spoonful of sugar into my tea. I hope that I'll be able to get my finger through the tiny handles on the delicate cup. Not that I've got very large hands for a man but I'm often ham-fisted with fragile objects.

Maud smiles. 'I gather this police inspector isn't winning any prizes in the school of manners and charm,' she says giving me a cheeky wink.

I chuckle at her remark and see a mischievous side to this straightlaced Mary Poppins figure. Dressed in a black skirt and a matching red jumper and cardigan, which I've heard Barbie call a twinset, she doesn't look much like the pretty governess played by Julie Andrews.

She picks up her cup of tea and sips it slowly with her brown brogues crossed at the ankles. And those brogues are certainly different to Mary's Poppins turned-out, red heeled shoes. I clear my thoughts away from the film, and smile, 'Yeah,' I say. 'You could put it like that.'

Not wanting to risk breaking the china cup I pick it up securely, hold it in the palm of my hand and slurp at the tea. The noise of police cars pulling up outside makes Liz jump up from her chair. Maud sits bolt upright and fingers her pearl necklace.

Ted Barker strides into the room followed closely by the blonde policewoman who had been with us on the day Audrey was found. The policewoman stands in the corner of the room with her arms behind her back and hands clasped together. I can tell she is only there to observe and witness events.

Liz introduces Ted to Maud. I get up too and shake his hand.

Gone is Ted's anorak. Today he is wearing a grey shirt and trousers. At least this shirt looks as though it has been ironed, I muse. We all sit down again, and I watch Maud's expressions. I can tell by the way she sniffs and pulls back her shoulders that she's not impressed. She probably thinks his appearance would look better with a tie and jacket and I have to agree. However, I know in CID detectives are allowed to wear casual clothes and reckon it could be worse – if Ted was younger, he could be dressed in jeans and T-shirt.

Ted refuses tea and begins to explain the news from the pathologist. 'Audrey has died from a suspicious death and did have a head injury which most likely happened after a fall to the ground,' he says sombrely. 'Therefore, she didn't drown in the sea.'

Maud murmurs, 'Thank God, for small mercies.'

The Inspector runs his hand over the long strand of hair at the front of his bald head and carries on, 'We are waiting for toxicology results and other tests coming back.'

Liz frowns. 'So, what does that mean - are you covering something up?'

Ted briskly shakes his head. 'No, we aren't,' he says. 'I'm simply trying to do my job and follow police procedures. Therefore, at this stage it doesn't mean to say that anyone else was involved.'

Liz looks distraught and I watch her try to pick up the tea cup but it rattles in the saucer. Maud reaches across to grip and steady her nieces hand.

Ted leans further forward to Liz and asks, 'And you're sure Audrey couldn't have walked down there? Maybe she tried and slipped then banged her head before falling onto the steps?'

'Good, God!' Liz exclaims. 'How many times do I have to say this? Mam could hardly walk around the garden on her own.'

Ted's feathers look ruffled to say the least, but he murmurs, 'We're just trying to get at the truth, Ms Mathews. Ordinarily, we would be checking personal belongings in clothes, handbags and mobile phone records. But in this case…'

Liz clatters the saucer back onto the coffee table. 'Okay, but I'm telling you the truth, and how can an old lady in a nightdress have belongings and a handbag?' She shouts. 'Mam wouldn't even know what a mobile phone is and, these questions are getting nothing short of repetitive!'

Ted clears his throat gruffly and continues to ask most of the questions he had yesterday. I watch Liz take a deep sigh.

Maud turns to Liz and pats the back of her hand. 'Have you answered these questions before, Elizabeth?'

Liz nods miserably. 'At least five times that I can remember.'

I can't stop myself and ask, 'So, Inspector, if Audrey wasn't capable of walking down to the causeway, it clearly means that someone else was involved because she had to get there somehow. Maybe she didn't fall and could have been pushed in some type of altercation?'

He bristles, ignores my question and doesn't even look in my direction. I have no choice but to accept his ignorance because after all, I am not a member of the family. Not even a close friend, I think and shrug my shoulders. I'm just someone trying to help.

Maud shuffles to the end of the chair. 'As far as I can see, Inspector, you aren't any further forward in ascertaining how my sister ended up dead in the sea.'

'Ah, but we are making progress,' he says nodding his head. 'We know there was no evidence of water in her lungs therefore, she definitely didn't die in the sea and was dead before she ended up on the steps.'

Ted gets up and looks down at them all. 'Well, of course, we'll be continuing with our enquiries, and I have my whole team looking through the CCTV cameras near the seafront,' he says. 'We are talking to people in the pub across the road to see if they saw anything at the roundabout and, of course, the few residents on St. Mary's Island. So, I'll report back to you, if and when there is more light to shed on the situation.'

I see the fury in Maud's eyes as she stands up to face him with her hands on her round hips. She purses her lips and I watch her inhale a deep breath. 'First, Inspector, my sister was not a situation and second, I'd like to know why you weren't concentrating your enquiries on the seafront when she was missing? In fact, I would like a written report into exactly how you are managing this investigation and, the name of your superior officer.'

Out of the corner of my eye I glance at the young policewoman who still hasn't moved or spoken. There's a little smirk playing around her lips as though she is enjoying Ted's discomfort at being outwitted by a bereaved relative.

Ted huffs and his sweaty cheeks glow even redder. 'I can assure you, Ms…'

Maud holds up her hand in front of his face. 'It's Mrs Davidson, actually. And I'm not convinced that my sister's death is being properly investigated. Therefore, I may contact your superior because from what I can see there's been nothing more done since my sister was found,' she says raising her voice. 'And, it wasn't even the police who found her!'

Ted turns on the heel of his scruffy shoes and I can almost feel the irritation coming off him in droves. 'Well, I don't think we can be blamed for not finding a confused elderly lady who had wandered off.'

There's a silence settles over both of them. I stroll over to Liz and squeeze her shoulders which are visibly trembling in a white silk blouse.

Ted starts to walk back down the hall and the young policewoman falls-in behind him.

Maud struts down the hallway after them both. 'My sister was suffering from poor mental health, Inspector and was in a vulnerable state,' she shouts. 'Did it not occur to your police officers to search down by the seafront as well as concentrating upon the caravan park?'

I hear him grunt and can see Ted is clearly stung by the criticism of his team. The policewoman's smirk is gone now and replaced with flaming red cheeks at Maud's accusation. Ted doesn't reply directly to Maud, but opens the back door and calls out, 'Goodbye, Ms Mathews, we'll be in touch.'

Maud heads directly to the drinks trolley in the corner of the lounge and takes out three shot glasses. She pours generous measures of brandy.

Liz bursts into huge sobs. 'I still can't believe she's gone – and in such horrible circumstances.'

I realise that Maud has poured out a brandy for me and I hurry across to her. 'Oh, thanks, Maud, but not for me. I don't drink spirits and I'm fine, really.'

She doesn't argue, but pours my measure into Liz's glass and whispers, 'Okay, but Elizabeth is in shock, and this will do her good.'

Maud carries the glass over to Liz and thrusts it at her. 'Here, drink this,' she says, and pulls out a clean white handkerchief from her sleeve to hand to Liz. 'And dry your eyes – crying isn't going to help anyone.'

I wince at her abruptness but know Liz will be more than used to her aunts brusque mannerisms.

Maud slumps back down into her chair and says, 'That Inspector is an absolute disgrace - fancy turning up to anyone's home without a tie and jacket.'

I smile knowing my first thoughts have been justified – uniforms and dress codes are important to old people.

She shakes her hand in front of me in a dismissive manner. 'No, Clive, there's no excuse for being slovenly, well, not in my books,' she says. 'It doesn't make for a good impression and hardly inspires confidence in people.'

I nod and decide to sum up the situation without of course using the same word which Ted had. 'So, all we know for sure is that Audrey's death is what they call unexplained. She definitely didn't die in the sea which is something to be grateful for at least,' I say. 'And she was dead before being dragged or carried there and placed on the steps which as I said before means someone else had to be involved in her death.'

Maud nods and I see Liz gulp at the brandy. The alcohol seems to be helping because she looks steadier and has stopped trembling.

Liz stutters, 'I mean, t…there were days that I could have cheerfully throttled her, but I wouldn't have,' she says. 'You don't do that sort of thing to an old lady – do you?'

I nod in agreement and take my leave to gushing thanks from both of them.

I protest. 'But I haven't done anything,' I say. 'In fact, I think Maud made more of an impression on the Inspector than I ever could.'

Both women smile as I wave goodbye, hurry out of the lodge and back along to Ashley Mews.

Chapter Twenty Two
Maud Davidson

Maud sighed as she lay on her sister's bed. The police and Clive were long gone, and Liz had actually dozed off to sleep in the big armchair in the lounge. She'd thrown a rug over her knowing how many sleepless nights her niece had endured. Maud figured it would do her good to nap.

She stretched out her arm over the quilt cover and thought of Audrey tucked-up safely in this bed where she had slept for years. A single tear escaped the corner of her eye and Maud wished she'd had time to see Audrey before she died. The official term was to pay one's respects but given the chance she would have told Audrey in her non-demonstrative way, how much she had always loved her.

Audrey had been her little sister when they were growing up and Maud had practically raised her when their parents were killed. Taking after their mother, they'd both been headstrong women determined to live their lives to the full. Which they had done. She had married a decent hardworking man from the south of the country and moved to Tiverton in Devon, when he was offered the foreman's job at Heathcoat Fabrics Ltd.

Both their lives had been like a rags-to-riches story. Maud had dragged herself up from being poor, living in a one room crummy flat in Seaton

*Sluice, to a high standard of living in a four
bedroomed detached house on Bakers Hill in
Tiverton. And, Audrey had fought tooth and nail
to develop the caravan park on a small piece of
land into what it was today.*

*Although the travelling distance had been a
problem in their later years her feelings hadn't
changed. Maud had felt as close to Audrey as
she'd always done. Of course, the last few years
had been difficult with telephone conversations
especially when Audrey hadn't known who she
was.*

*Maud sighed, she had to hand it to Elizabeth –
she'd been a real star looking after her mam so
well. In fact, Maud had always been a little
envious of their mother and daughter
relationship knowing Sheila would never give up
her travels to stay home and look after her.
Maud winced, it was a sad thing to admit but
true all the same. However, it had been a
comfort to know that Audrey hadn't wanted for a
thing. Liz had taken just as good care of her
sister as she would have done herself.*

*Turning over to face the window she closed her
eyes for a few minutes. If only her sister had
died in normal circumstances, it would have
been easier to prepare for the funeral. Both her
and Elizabeth knew Audrey's wishes and where
they were to lay her to rest.*

*But what had happened? And who had done
this? She had to know if someone had
intentionally hurt Audrey, after all she'd spent*

much of her life protecting her sister. And, there were still so many unanswered questions. Especially as to how Audrey had gotten herself down to the causeway on her own as the Inspector seemed to think. Maud didn't know much about investigations and unexplained deaths, but this whole case had a bad smell of shoddy policework.

When Clive had summed up the circumstances and reality of their predicament, it made more sense that someone else had been involved. She grimaced remembering that bloody causeway of old times and the shenanigans that had gone on down there.

Maud shook them resolutely from her mind and thought of Clive instead. She remembered her first impressions of him. When Elizabeth had told her how much he'd helped, she had been immediately suspicious. Was he a chancer looking for a cash hand-out? In her experience, most people expected some type of reward for their help in any circumstance. And, not many people nowadays gave their time and assistance freely. However, within a few minutes she'd decided Clive was in fact, simply a good decent man that wanted to help poor Elizabeth being on her own.

Maud started when there was a soft tap on the bedroom door and knew she had dozed off to sleep. 'Come in, Elizabeth,' she called. 'Really, there's no need to knock – this is your home not mine.'

Her niece slid around the door and perched on the end of the bed. She was holding what looked like an old card photograph in her hand and Maud could tell there was a reason for her coming.

'Sorry,' Elizabeth said and yawned. 'I wasn't sure if you'd fallen asleep like I've just done.'

Maud shuffled herself further up on the pillows and waited. She looked at her niece's tormented face and saw so much of Audrey in her. And her own daughter, Sheila who she missed dreadfully every time she went off to work in far-flung places of the world.

'I'll get up and make some tea,' Maud said.

Elizabeth stretched and cranked her neck. 'Nooo, not yet, Aunt Maud. I've been wanting to ask this since you arrived yesterday and can't wait any longer.'

Explaining how she'd found the very old photograph under Audrey's pillow, she handed it to her. 'Do you know who this soldier is?'

She took the photograph and reached for her glasses on the bedside table. Putting them on Maud stared at the soldier and gasped. Her heart sank while all the old memories filled her mind and whirled with possibilities.

Maud could say she didn't know, but that admission would never fool Elizabeth – she was too smart to be fobbed off with lies. She sighed heavily. 'You know, all I can say is that sometimes it's best not to know and it's easier if things are left unsaid.'

Elizabeth shrugged. 'Maybe, but I want to know. If this man was important enough for Mam to keep his photo under her pillow, then I'd like to find out about him?'

She knew Elizabeth would insist upon the truth because it was what Audrey would have done and after all, she was her mother's daughter. 'But you've had a horrible three days and are still traumatised by losing your mam,' she said. 'How about we leave it for now and in a few months, I'll tell you all about him then?'

However, her niece vehemently shook her head and pursed those thin lips. 'No! Aunt Maud – tell me now.'

Maud could see her sister's likeness and it made her want to cry - she swallowed a dry lump in her throat. However, she nodded in acknowledgement of defeat and took another deep breath. 'Well, before I tell you about him, Elizabeth, you must remember that seventy years ago the world was a very different place to what it is now.'

Elizabeth shuffled further up the bed towards her as though she didn't want to miss a single word of what she had to say.

Maud continued, 'If you remember your mam and I were brought up along the coast in Seaton Sluice and we both worked at Seaton Delaval Hall. I got my job first in the kitchens and a year later Audrey started as a cleaner,' she said.

Elizabeth nodded encouragingly as if to say keep going.

Licking her dry lips, Maud knew what she had to say would be upsetting. 'Well at the time your mam was sixteen when she met one of the German soldiers. I didn't know anything about him of course until it was too late, and she came to me in tears because she'd missed her monthly.'

She didn't get any more words out when Elizabeth cried aloud, 'You mean she was pregnant and had a baby with this soldier?'

Maud stared at her eyes which were huge like big saucers. Two massive shocks in three days were enough to upset anyone, but Elizabeth would take it in her stride just like Sheila would - the Mathews women were nothing, if not resilient. She nodded. 'Er, yes, but as I said before things were very different back then and it was a total disgrace to be pregnant and a single woman. So, when the soldier went home to Germany, I went to see the priest and he helped with arrangements. He paid the £5 fee because we didn't live in their area, and your mam went to a nursing home in Carlisle. She had the baby and stayed for two years working in the laundry which was part of the deal. We never knew if the baby was given up for adoption, but we hoped so…'

Elizabeth's face twisted into new avenues of grief and pain. She scrunched up her eyebrows and cried, 'Oh, no, poor Mam!'

Maud could almost see Elizabeth's brain working through the news when she jumped up from the bed. 'So, you mean to tell me that I have a half-brother or sister somewhere?'

Silenced settled between them and Maud nodded. 'Yes, it was a boy,' she muttered. 'But don't ask me what happened to him because I don't know and neither did your mam.'

Shaking her head at Maud, Elizabeth tutted. 'But how could you do that to her?'

Maud braced herself knowing she'd be seen as the big bad wolf in what they'd done. 'It was for the best and at the time I'd been glad that we could get it taken care of so that it wouldn't ruin her life and mine.'

Elizabeth took the photograph back, jumped up and left the bedroom clashing the door shut with a bang.

Chapter Twenty Three

I'm in the pool swimming in an effort to clarify my thoughts. I'm doing breast stroke in long even movements and dipping my head up at each thrust through the water. I remember the conversation with Ted earlier and know I'm not wrong because his version of events just doesn't add up.

I think through different scenarios with each stroke relishing in the water which is cooler at this time of day. It's even more refreshing than in a morning. Apart from another woman doing lengths on the other side of the pool it is peaceful without the children's noise and antics.

When I'd left the lodge, my antenna had been on red alert remembering the word that Liz had used - throttle. Could she really have lost all control and indeed hurt her mam? Or was this just a phrase that she used in throes of extreme frustration? Because that's what it must be like looking after someone who was continually confused.

I've read on the Alzheimer's website that as the disease progresses patients become more agitated with worry. The agitation may cause them to pace around in a restless manner and result in sleeplessness and sometimes aggression.

Could Liz have just snapped and unintentionally pushed Audrey causing her to fall? Which would, of course, be accidental, or did Liz cause her mam actual harm? However, if she had done this – how would she carry Audrey down to the causeway? There was no car and Liz wasn't a big strapping sixty year old. She was thin and didn't look as though she could carry an old lady. Maybe she got someone to take her away – one of the groundsmen perhaps? Or the nightshift security officer? I shake my head knowing I'm grasping at straws.

An author friend often uses the theory, to find out how a woman has died you have to find out how she lived, and I've applied this concept in my book. My fictional detective, Jason Jennings finds out about the student's life during his investigations.

So, I decide to apply this to Audrey. I know how she lived now suffering from Alzheimer's and, how she'd lived in the past. She had devoted her life to building up the caravan park. She has one daughter and a sister and niece in Devon. Audrey had made a good amount of money and even after having the lodge built from scratch, she was leaving Liz a hefty nest-egg to retire whenever she decided it was her time.

I turn at the end of the pool and feel my leg muscles pulling. Another ten lengths, I think and realise I don't know much about Liz's father, Duncan. All Liz told me was that they'd never heard from him since Mam divorced him. Apparently, he'd been cruel and, as Liz had put it, too handy with his fists.

Counting down lengths at number five, I tut thinking about domestic abuse and how men assault and hit women. I've never hit anyone in my life and wouldn't know how to throw an effective punch like other men can. And especially not at a woman.

Barbie had once said, 'My dad used to say there was much better ways to get what you wanted from a woman without raising your fists.'

I smile knowing this is true and how he must have been a wise man. I chuckle thinking of Barbie's Mam - she wouldn't have stood for any type of abuse from him. Perhaps a little like Audrey wouldn't. Northern women have a reputation for being strong and resilient although this doesn't always factor against ill-treatment. Emotional control can be just as damaging as physical abuse.

I count length three and frown. If Duncan was around the same age as Audrey, he would be ninety now, that's if he was still alive. And, if so, would a man of his age travel down from Scotland to seek revenge upon his ex-wife and daughter? The motive was there if he demanded a share of the caravan parks profits and Liz's nest-egg, but it sounded flimsy, and I decide not.

While I turn for the last length, I decide to ask a few questions from the main people associated with Liz. In fact, all of the caravan residents that I've met so far. Of course, there's loads more on the park that we could be equally suspicious about but because I haven't met them all, I can start with the ones I do know.

Towelling myself dry in the cubicle, I feel energised after the swim and decide to start with the most important question, where was everyone between 11pm and 4am on that night.

The definition on Google tells me, an alibi is a claim or piece of evidence that one was elsewhere when an act, typically a criminal one, is alleged to have taken place. And, if you have an alibi that is backed by tangible evidence, you may be able to escape criminal charges or a conviction.

I know that proving this nowadays is easier than in the past. Even if you were alone, like I was on Monday night, and made a social media post, you can use this as an alibi. Your phone GPS can track the location and this data can be accessed by your telecom provider when necessary. I remember how Barbie placed a photo of us on Facebook and I had answered with a cheeky comment, so I figure this should be all the proof I would need.

I think of my own Jason Jennings and know he has checked and double-checked the alibis for his suspects and interested parties who were around the murdered student in Durham. I've written air-tight defences for her family and friends to aid Jason discounting them from his enquiries and the police investigation.

I wonder if Ted Barker has done this? Has he made a list of people to interview who could take Audrey down to the causeway? Does Ted know where everyone was that night - staff and groundsmen included? Does he know who the regulars are that come every weekend and stay for most of the summer months?

I'm thinking of Celia and Jim and their two friends in the gin & tonic brigade. Have they more friends who have known Liz and Audrey just as long - and should I question them too?

I remember what I was doing later that night when Audrey wandered outside of the lodge although there were no witnesses because I was dreaming about making love to Barbie. I can remember the exact details of my dream. We were lying on the beach sun bathing. Barbie in her little green bikini and well, I'll leave the rest to everyone's imagination.

I Google police procedures and read through posts. I smile at one comment which says, relatives should be dealt with calmly and sensitively in order to minimise distress. Hmm, I wonder if I should print this out to show Ted? Obviously, he doesn't know about this or has forgotten.

When a body is discovered in a public place the coroner will ask for police to gather information which determines the difference between an unexplained or suspicious death. I remember Ted had used the word unexplained down at the causeway, but obviously after the post mortem the name changed to suspicious.

At the scene, police should record all of the circumstances in their notebooks. Were there signs of a struggle? They should check the position of the body and a detailed description and hope they did all of this at the scene. I figure even though I don't have a hundred percent confidence in the police, the coroner's team did appear to be efficient and professional.

Chapter Twenty Four

Liz

Liz had felt panic rising again in her chest and her heart rate quicken when Aunt Maud had told her about Mam having a baby and the adoption. After seeing her dead at the causeway, the feelings of panic had settled and had been replaced with overwhelming grief. Now the panic was raging around again at full force and Liz took long slow deep breaths in and out as Clive had shown her. Eventually she felt her heart begin to slow down which steadied her.

Whether it had been bad mannered to leave her aunt or not she'd had to get out of the bedroom and be alone with her thoughts which now tumbled mercilessly.

Maud had looked upset when she told her about the Carlisle nursing home. However, Liz could tell by the look on her aunt's face that she hadn't known what happened to the baby boy and Liz believed she was telling the truth. When Maud had pursed her lips, it meant there was nothing more to say on the matter. Liz knew it was exactly what Mam would have said and the likeness of the two sisters felt comforting but sad at the same time because she was no longer there.

Lying on her bed, Liz stared at the ceiling and thought, somewhere in the world she had a half-brother. She sighed knowing that there could also be more family who were living their lives as Liz was doing completely unaware that either existed.

Why hadn't Mam told her about the baby? How could she have kept this a secret for over seventy years? Liz had thought their mother-daughter relationship had been very close, but obviously not, and wiped a tear from the corner of her eye. A small amount of resentment built up against Mam for doing this to her. She knew other people would excuse it as an oversight because of her memory loss but Audrey had only suffered this in the last few years. Surely Mam could have told her when she became a woman and understood these things.

Perhaps, as Maud had said back then it was shameful, but less so in the 70s, 80s and 90s, and nowadays there was no shame in single motherhood whatsoever. As her daughter, she wouldn't have thought any less of Audrey for finding herself pregnant aged sixteen. Liz would have felt more pity than shame to any young girl in that situation, even now.

Liz cast her mind back and remembered a couple of occasions in her twenties when she'd had a near miss but thankfully it had simply been late periods. She hadn't told Mam because it would have worried her unnecessarily. However, Liz did recall how scared she'd felt at the thought of being pregnant and alone.

She had talked about this with her teenage friends at school and they'd been terrified of their mothers, but she had never been frightened of Audrey. Liz had always known Mam would support her whatever the outcome. So, if she knew this, how could Mam not tell her that she'd been through it all herself?

Shaking her head, she wished Mam was still here to talk about it all. She wanted her old Mam, not the demented Mam who had no realms of reality. She rolled over onto her side and stroked a finger down the cheek of Audrey in a photograph on her bedside table. It felt like an ache that would never go away and knew she hadn't even started to grieve for her yet.

Finding the remote control, she switched on the TV. Liz remembered a program she'd watched last week and found it on catch-up - DNA Family Secrets. Was this only a week ago when her life was mundane and normal looking after Mam and the caravan park? It seemed unreal and she pressed play.

Liz watched how a seventy-eight year old Liverpool lady asked the presenter if they could trace her father. The lady had been told when she was nineteen by a family friend that her dad was not her biological father. Her real father had been an American GI in 1943. The lady's mother would never talk about it before she died being too ashamed because he was African American - therefore, she thought he was lost without trace.

Liz breathed out heavily and sighed. Here was someone in a similar situation to herself although it was her brother not her father.

The Liverpool lady's own sons were very talented, musical, and she too had loved dancing. The lady had wondered over the yeas where this talent came from and had many questions. Did she have any of her real father's traits? She had found not knowing very hard to cope with. Who was she and where had she come from in America? She'd said, 'Even when the knowing is not good, it's still better than not knowing at all.'

Of course, Liz hadn't experienced any of these feelings as yet because she had only found out a few hours ago, but already she could understand how not knowing would torture a person. The show then filmed a sequence with the top geneticist who works with DNA and gave the interviewer her statistics.

Liz grabbed a notebook to jot down the facts and swallowed hard. The page had word games on that she used to play with Mam in the early days of diagnosis to keep her mind active. She pushed these thoughts aside determined to concentrate.

The geneticist said, 'It was possible to upload one's own DNA onto world-wide data bases which could link not only grandparents and parents but also first and second cousins if their DNA was registered. This formed the link where closest living relatives could be traced. Apparently, there were thirty million DNA results registered.'

*The program matched up the Liverpool ladies'
father in America and she switched off the TV.*

*Liz sucked in a quick breath at the statistics
she'd written in the notebook - it was a massive
subject. So, if she did decide to trace her brother
it seemed to be relatively easy after submitting
her DNA onto the data bases.*

*She bit her lip – would Mam want her to do
this? They were respecting all of Audrey's
wishes and carrying out everything she'd asked
for at the funeral. But what happened
afterwards? When Mam wasn't here, and Maud
had gone home to Tiverton? Liz would be all
alone and she shivered.*

*It dawned upon Liz that Mam would never
know if she did try to trace her half-brother.
That was, of course, if he was still alive? She
sighed heavily – the Mathews ladies obviously
lived long lives, but her half-brother would be
seventy eight and could have died.*

*Liz heard Maud in the bathroom getting ready
for bed and sighed. It seemed strange to hear
someone else in the lodge and she wished with
all her heart that it could be Mam. Liz knew she
had been abrupt with Maud and remembered
Audrey's old saying, 'Never go to bed on an
argument.'*

*She headed out of her bedroom to apologise to
Maud knowing Mam would want her to keep the
peace.*

Chapter Twenty Five

I leave the pool and walk past Amber's caravan. I hear a man's loud voice shouting and joking. The side door swings open and Amber steps outside with a black bag of rubbish.

'Hey, Clive,' she says.

Obviously, Kieran had arrived and certainly put a smile back on her face again. In fact, I could cheerfully say, she is glowing. Her skinny jeans are back and a low-cut pink T-Shirt compliments how she is evidently feeling – bright and cheerful.

I too, feel happy not just for Amber's sake but also for my own. Hopefully she'll stop flirting with me now. Although Barbie had made a joke of the flirtation and I'd gone along with her - it had made me feel uncomfortable.

I stop and ask, 'Hiya, how's things going?'

A slim guy puts his head around the door amidst giggling from the girls behind him and I introduce myself.

There's stubble on his chin which tells me he needs a shave, but he seems to have shaved his head instead because it's as smooth as a baby. Two dragon tattoos are snaked down both his arms which are visible in the sleeveless vest. He's wearing Doc Martin boots and I reckon his feet must be hot as I look down at my flipflops.

I step forward and shake his hand while Amber tells Kieran how I've been helping Liz after the awful death of her mother.

Kieran says, 'Yeah, it sounds like a bad business, poor old woman.'

Now he's spoken I can detect his broad Irish accent and decide he looks like a tired, worn-out, Johnny Depp. I look at the blankness in his eyes and am immediately reminded of my dad and how he used to look when he was on a drug bender. It's a certain blankness that says there's a light on inside, but nobody is in there. I figure Kieran is around my age or maybe a little older, but drugs do that to a person – they age you rapidly.

Kieran smiles at Amber when she pokes him playfully in his ribs. His teeth are discoloured, and he has huge black eyes. I reckon Amber's oldest girl is about ten so this means she must have met Kieran when he was in his early twenties and looked like the younger Johnny Depp. I can see how Amber would have been totally bowled over by him.

Whilst looking at them both I wonder how to ascertain their alibis without seeming nosey. I sigh, where are my powers of a detective questioning when I need them the most?

The best I come up with is, 'So, we've been having some lovely sunshine this week although it was cloudy this morning,' I say. 'But you seem to have brought the good weather with you – did you get here last night?'

Kieran furrows his eyebrows and I feel a shiver run up my spine. Not one of my bad instinct shivers but a warning to be careful. Although I think he looks tired and worn out, I think of an old saying and know I wouldn't want to cross swords with him. Apart from looking like he can handle himself, people who use drugs are often volatile and highly strung.

Amber looks a little shifty fiddling with a zip on her jean pocket. 'Kieran has been working further along the coast and got here at nine – so we've been catching up all night in the caravan,' she says.

Kieran pulls her none too gently against him and squeezes her right arm. Even at a distance I can see his grip is enough to leave a bruise. He puts his other hand on her small bottom and grabs it firmly pulling her up against his pelvis. He stares at me over her shoulder with a warning look in his big eyes.

'Don't be too long with the rubbish,' he says and grunts. 'I need you again in the bedroom.'

This sickens me. I turn to walk away as Kieran thumps up the step inside and clashes the caravan door behind him.

I feel insulted but this is quickly overridden with concern for Amber. She bends down to pick up the black sack from the grass and hurries over to the bin area. I stride across after her. Closer up, I notice other bruises on her left arm when her T-shirt has rucked up.

Temper flares inside and I want to shout at her, for goodness sake, why are you putting up with this? You're such a beautiful woman you could have any decent, loving man instead of this moron. But I know my rant will fall on deaf ears.

'Are you okay?' I ask and look into her face. Gone is the earlier glowing look. It's replaced with fear in her eyes and an apprehensive glance over her shoulder towards the caravan door. I know she is scared of him.

'Oh, yes,' she says. 'He's grouchy today because we had one too many cans last night - look, I'll have to get back inside.'

She drops the sack into one of the huge green receptacles and says, 'But he's lovely when he hasn't got a drink in him.'

I nod and continue around the corner to my caravan door thinking all the while. He obviously has a temper and ill-treats Amber. And, come to think of it, he hadn't been none too friendly towards me, either. But did this make him violent and abusive to other people?

I pull out the key from my jacket and wonder. I know he only arrived on the caravan park last night, but Amber said he had been working further along the coast this last week. So, could he have been around the park on Monday night? And, is he the type of guy who would push Audrey over on the steps? Would he actually do that to an elderly lady and if so, why her? Was it a freak accident that Audrey was just there and filled with booze or drugs he had a run-in with her? Or is Amber telling the truth and Kieran didn't turn up until last night?

Chapter Twenty Six

Amber

Amber is scared. She knows that Kieran has been lying to her and doesn't know what to do about him. He's taken the girls down to the pool with the excuse that it'll give her time to tidy-up. She looks around the caravan at unmade beds, toys scattered, and dishes piled up in the sink then sighs feeling unable to move – she's exhausted.

The image of him when they first met comes into her mind and how she'd hung on his every word. Back then she had no reason to mistrust or doubt anything he'd said to her but now he made it hard for her to believe in him.

When they were first together, he only did a little weed on special occasions, and it never affected his temperament or working ability. He never lost a day's work, but this had progressed onto stronger stuff and now he did lose jobs, although this didn't seem to bother his boss on the construction site. He paid him by the day with cash-in-hand. And as Kieran had always said, 'I'm a skilled builder – I'll always find work.'

But would he? The coffee in her mug is lukewarm and she gulps it down feeling the need of caffeine to spur her into action. From his grand arrival at the caravan, he'd let a couple of things slip after three cans of lager.

'We've been in Whitley Bay since Monday morning when I finished work on Sunday night at the site,' he'd said. 'And then went on a bender with my mates.'

She'd nodded and felt the usual sense of apprehension when he mentioned the bender. It had become more common over the last six months, and she knew what it entailed.

'Yeah,' he'd cackled. 'We had a great time with some decent stuff and enough booze to empty the brewery.'

Amber took the word stuff to mean drugs. And if she was totally honest with herself the addiction to drugs frightened her more than the alcohol. She felt weary and sore after the bombardment in bed yesterday. Gone was making love with tender endearments that they used to share. There was very little affection left on his behalf - although not from her. Sometimes when they were coupled together, she kept her eyes closed and remembered how caring and tender he used to be. Now it was just a primeval act.

Filling the sink with warm soapy water she began to wash dishes and let her thoughts drift to when he'd knocked loudly on the caravan door at two in the morning. She'd got a shock at the noise and staggered through the caravan towards the door.

Kieran had slumped down on the sofa. He'd had muck on his jeans as though he had been kneeling in dirt. However, messy clothes were a *regular thing when he went on a bender with his mates. She knew they sat around make-shift fires in fields or on the beach with homeless people taking and selling drugs.*

Shivering in revulsion, she had stripped the jeans from his legs while he'd said, 'I tripped and fell on the damp grass.'

He had opened her bathrobe and one thing led to another.

Amber stacked the dishes and dried her hands wondering where he'd been staying with these so-called friends in Whitley Bay. She didn't know if there were hostels here like there was in Middlesborough. However, one incident came to her mind which made Amber think he could have been up in Whitley Bay town centre.

Jayden had said on Monday when they were getting ice creams on the beach that she thought she'd seen her daddy. Amber had dismissed this as a fantasy because she often made up stories about people. However, maybe her daughter hadn't made this one up? She picked up Jayden's favourite lion toy from the lounge floor and hugged it to her chest. Amber sighed, now she was doubting her children because of his deceit.

Had Kieran seen them on the beach? She shrugged her shoulders knowing that if he'd been out of his mind on drugs then he wouldn't have approached them because he might not have even recognised his daughters. How shameful was that, she thought and felt tears sting her eyes while picking up the rest of the toys.

She headed into the twin bedroom and fluffed up the quilts with her mind racing. If Kieran had been near the beach on Monday, had he staggered down to the caravan park looking for her in his druggie stupor and got lost? She knew Kieran was capable of anything when he was high on drugs because she'd seen him in the past.

Audrey came into her mind, and she shuddered. Had Kieran wandered around the park on Monday night? If he'd seen Audrey and thought she had money, then maybe? She gave a small cry of alarm and began to tremble. She stuffed the end of the quilt against her mouth – was he actually capable of coshing an old lady over the head? Noooo, he wouldn't do that – would he?

She flopped down on the end of the bed and took long slow deep breaths trying to steady herself. She was letting her imagination run riot with the pressure of having him here. And that's what it was now – hassle and upset. Amber decided, having him in her life was no fun anymore. The excitement and buzz had long since gone and the strain far outweighed any pleasure. She knew it was coming to the end and when she got home it was going to finish for good.

Amber thought about yesterday and how rude he'd been to Clive who was such a nice, decent man. Kieran had humiliated her in front of him and later at the bin area Clive had been so concerned about her that she'd had to fight back tears. She swallowed hard remembering how she had told Clive and then later, the police, that Kieran had arrived at 9pm. She didn't know why she'd lied about the time because it had nothing to do with Audrey's disappearance and subsequent death.

Biting the side of her fingernail, she frowned. It was a habit she'd long since grown out of, but now she was frightened. Amber had never been in trouble before with the police and when they'd asked for her whereabouts on Monday night, she had become flustered. Amber had stressed that she had been alone in the caravan with the girls and that Kieran hadn't arrived then. But now her stomach churned - had that looked even more suspicious?

Suddenly, she heard the girls giggling and Kieran's voice singing loudly to one of their favourite songs. They were coming back up to the caravan. Instantly the heckles on the back of her neck rose and she swallowed a big lump in her throat. She felt jumpy around him now – not knowing what he would do next.

Chapter Twenty Seven

After leaving Amber I'd got back to the caravan and wrote a paragraph thinking of a character like Kieran. I imagined his face and described him, 'He looks aggressive. Is solitary with no friends. A real loner. People are tense around him. He manipulates Amber and kids. Their lives are regimented, and he rules by the power of violence.

Later, I had talked to Barbie on my mobile with amazing news that she was hoping to finish her contract earlier than expected and join me at the caravan. When I gave her an update on Audrey's death, she'd said, 'Oh, Clive, please be careful with this situation now.'

I'd heard the wariness in her voice and imagined her little eyebrows drawn together. The last thing I wanted to do was alarm her, so I soothed, 'Oh, I will – don't worry. I know when to step back and leave a situation before it escalates.'

The relief in her voice had been audible and I'd known her mind was at ease. After we'd whispered sweet nothings to each other and good night wishes, I had clicked off my mobile.

Now, I am pulling on my jeans and trainers again and my thick fisherman sweater. It's just gone ten and I'm heading out to see if I can find the night-time security officer.

Every night since I arrived, I've either been writing or lying watching TV until midnight, but I've set aside this time to see where the security officer had been on the night Audrey was taken. Of which I'm sure now - someone must have taken her down to that causeway.

***

Locking the door, I pass by Amber's caravan, but all is silent and in darkness. What I'd told Barbie was true because I won't get involved with domestic arguments and I do know how to walk away from a dodgy situation. Unless of course Amber and the gigglers were being threatened or attacked and then I would step in, call the police and try to protect them.

Barbie's Mam knitted the fisherman's sweater, and it feels cosy around my neck against the chilly sea breeze which has picked up now. Instead of immediately walking down to the Entertainment Centre I turn right and head up to the top of Ash Mews looking around to see if I can spot the security officer.

The area is quiet, but well-lit with intermittent streetlights and I notice most people have their small outside lights switched on. I only pass one dog walker who wishes me goodnight while I continue walking. I head down to the reception in a semi-circle looking along each row of caravans for the security van.

The van is actually parked up outside the reception doors and I see a man sitting inside at the wheel. I stop by the driver's window and wave at him. The man who looks to be in his late fifties winds down his window and smiles.

'Hello, there,' I say. 'Have you a few minutes to spare?'

I peer inside the van and see sandwiches opened on a piece of tin foil and realise he must be on his break. A small stripey flask is balanced on the cup holder.

'Well,' he says and wrinkles his eyebrows as though irritated at my interruption.

His face is thin, and his fair hair seems to twinkle under the street light above our heads. He asks, 'Is there a problem on the park?'

I realise he thinks I'm going to report an issue. 'Oh, no, there's nothing wrong,' I say and give him a big smile. 'I'm just making enquiries on behalf of Liz.'

He lifts his chin at the sound of her name and turns to face me. I see that the badge on his high-viz jacket says, John Edwards, Security Officer.

He nods and looks me up and down. 'Are you with the police?'

'Not exactly, John,' I say. 'But Liz knows I'm helping by talking with staff on the park. And I just wondered if you were on duty last Monday night when Audrey disappeared?'

I can smell what I'm sure is corned beef in his sandwiches and see him glance at them longingly. 'Last Monday?' He says.

I can almost see the cogs of his brain tick over when he rubs his jaw and I nod at him.

'Aye, I was working, but can't say that I saw anything of Audrey that night.'

I smile and know I've got his attention now. I need to find out his routine on a nightly basis. 'So, do you usually patrol around by the lodge, or do you only drive down if there's a problem?'

He leans forward and pulls out a clip board with Log Book written on the top. He licks his finger and scrolls back the pages. 'I patrol every inch of the grounds but must admit there's never much going on down the back where the lodge is situated.'

I'd love to lean over and take the book to look at myself, but I take a deep breath knowing my interference will irritate him. 'Oh, wow, I can see how organised you are – this is amazing, John,' I say and watch him preen.

'Aye, well, I like to keep a tidy ship, as Liz often says.'

I can see he is tracking down the entries on Monday night with his long thin finger. 'Nope, the only thing that happened was a missing dog, but we found it shivering underneath the next caravan and that was up the top end of the park in dahlia section.'

I nod and smile again. 'Okay, and is there an entry for the exact time you were busy up there?'

'Yes, it was at 12.30pm and I returned to reception for my break at 1.30am.'

I jiggle this around in my mind knowing this was the time when Audrey was probably wandering in the garden. Unfortunately, John would have been at the opposite end of the caravan park, so even if there had been an altercation he wouldn't have heard or seen anything.

'Oh, right,' I say. 'And did you tell the police this when they interviewed you?'

John screws up his face and rubs his jaw again. 'The police?' He asks. 'I haven't been spoken to by the police – I've never seen them.'

I take a deep intake of breath and ask one last question which I've heard repeatedly on TV crime shows. 'Thanks, John and can I just ask, do you know of anyone who would want to harm Liz or Audrey?'

'Harm them?' He says. 'Now who would want to do a thing like that – they're the salt of the earth – best bosses I've ever had.'

I nod, thank him again and wander back around to Ashley Mews. I'm horrified to think the police haven't even taken a statement from him. I suppose they'll have checked John's log book, but this isn't as good as face to face interviewing. Thankfully, I decide it wouldn't have mattered because there's nothing to report and he hadn't seen anything. However, I think of Maud's words, shoddy policework and sigh - she has this right on the button.

Chapter Twenty Eight

The next morning, I lie in bed deep in thought. I can't find the energy to spring up out of bed and hit the day head-on. This is unusual for me as I like to think of myself as a morning person. Most days it is when I can write with clarity rather than in the evening. I have author friends who are the opposite and start to write mid-afternoon then continue until midnight. I've never been able to do this – it's when I feel the most tired.

I rustle my legs between the sheets feeling too hot and restless because I'm missing Barbie. I turn onto my side and as often happens when I am on holiday, I struggle to remember which day of the week it is. I decide upon Friday. Like many other people, I found this a real problem during the pandemic when we were in lock-down when every day seemed the same. Unbelievably, it's a week since I arrived at the caravan park and so much has happened - mainly Audrey's suspicious death.

I swing my legs out of bed eventually knowing that on top of completing the chapter I'd started yesterday, I have to talk with my caravan neighbours about their alibis. Filling the kettle to make coffee I rephrase my thinking. I don't have to ascertain everyone's alibi's, but I want to because in my own small way I'll be helping Liz. And, of course, I want to know the answer too. I need to know what happened to Audrey in the garden outside their lodge. I'm convinced now that she heard or saw somebody outside which made her open the door.

I frown and settle outside on the veranda with my laptop open. I sip the hot coffee which along with hot buttered toast revives me somewhat.

I think of Jason Jennings and remember the paragraph I'd scribbled in Cullercoats.

'Jason has arrested his suspect for the student murder and although he was a big man with a history of violent assault, he'd been no match for Jason when his heckles were up and blood had pumped through every vein in his body. Jason could have felt intimidated, but he had youth, agility, and surprise on his side.

I smile unable to stop myself comparing him to Ted Barker who, although is much older, doesn't seem to have any type of emotion on his side. He appears to be devoid of any feeling. Or perhaps that is just his professional work outlook and at home he is a jolly party-goer. I grin at the thought of Ted raving to dance music with his comb-over hair.

There's no sun this morning, but the air feels humid, and I glance to my right noting Amber and the gigglers are not out and about as yet. Just as I drain the coffee from my mug, I hear Celia call my name and jerk my head to the left.

This couldn't have been a more opportune moment and know I can ask about an alibi for Monday. I saunter to the edge of the white railings.

'Hey, Celia,' I say. 'How's it going?'

'Oh, okay, I guess but isn't it awful news about poor Audrey?'

I realise that I haven't spoken to them since the day we searched the caravan park for Audrey and nod my head. 'Yep, it's tragic,' I say automatically looking behind her for Jim. They're usually together or at least not far from each other. 'Let's hope the police can find out exactly what's happened.'

Celia looks tired. Her face is downturned, and she certainly doesn't look like her chirpy busy-bodied self. I notice the green tracksuit she is wearing looks as tired as she does and wonder if there's something else bothering her other than the sad news.

She says, 'Yes, I've been feeling very unsettled since Tuesday when they found the old woman down at the causeway. So much so, that we were thinking of going home especially if there's a murderer or kidnapper in our midst.'

Celia rests her hands on top of the white railings, and I can see they're trembling. I feel sorry for her and am surprised at her reaction. I'd have thought she would have been full of gossip about Audrey with the police in attendance. I try to comfort her. 'Oh, I'm sure there's no need to worry so much, Celia and if there was such a murderer he'll be long gone by now.'

She nods. 'That's exactly what James says, but I suppose you never know, and I don't feel as safe here as I do at home with our secure lever-locks on the doors and windows.'

I try a reassuring smile and decide, rather than asking a direct question about an alibi it would be best to slip it into the conversation. 'I can understand that,' I say. 'But it's been so hot I've been sleeping with the bedroom window open. Although I must admit on that Monday night, I never heard a thing from up here on Ash Mews.'

Celia tuts and shakes her head. 'Nor did I, but we'd had our friends here until midnight playing bridge and by the time I'd cleared away supper dishes, it was later than usual when we got into bed.'

I smile amazed that people still play bridge in this day and age. I know it's a card game but can't help thinking that it sounds more like something from a murder-mystery weekend in a stately home rather than a caravan in Whitley Bay. While I'm deciding whether to make a funny comment to try and cheer her up, I hear Rusty barking and look down the side of their caravan. He scampers up to the railings and puts his front paws on the ledge. I lean right over and tickle his ears.

Jim is not far behind him and comes up to my veranda. He reaches up and we shake hands. His hand is sweaty, and his cheeks are pink. I figure it's probably due to the heat and brisk walk.

'Hey, Jim, enjoy your walk?' I ask and watch Rusty wagging his tail furiously. 'I was just saying to Celia that I hadn't seen either of you since they found Audrey.'

Jim averts his gaze away from me at the mention of Audrey and looks towards Celia. He doesn't answer but says to Celia, 'I got pork chops for dinner.'

I look at his face and decide he looks tormented. It's the only word I think of to describe the look on his face. 'Oh, sorry,' I say. 'You guy's must be upset because you and your bridge playing friends have known the Mathews for years, haven't you?'

Celia nods. 'Yeah, they have and longer than us, really.'

I watch Jim's neck flush and he tugs at his ear. There's an accusatory tone in his voice when he says, 'And I've heard that you've been helping the police by questioning people?'

Ah, I think, that's why he obviously feels uncomfortable around me, but I smile and say, 'No, not the police, but I've tried to help Liz, and from what I've seen they need all the help they can get!'

Celia's face brightens for the first time. 'Yes, we heard they're not quite The Flying Squad.'

Jim pulls out his vape and puffs on it hard. 'Well, the police haven't spoken to us but there again, there's no reason why they should because we didn't see anything that night.'

He's now on defensive mode and I watch him draw his shoulders up nearly to his chin.

Celia leans forward to Jim and asks, 'Didn't you take Rusty out for a walk at midnight on Monday because he wouldn't settle - or was that Tuesday night?'

Jim snaps at her. 'It was Tuesday night!'

Celia pouts. 'No, it wasn't,' she snipes back. 'It was Monday after our friends left and I was doing the dishes.'

I feel a flutter of excitement in my belly and jump straight in with a question. 'Did you see anyone hanging around, Jim? Or anything that didn't look right?'

Jim shuffles his feet and looks down at Rusty then puffs again on his vape. 'Well, the only thing I saw was the blinds open at Dennis's caravan side window but that's hardly suspicious – it's just that they're usually closed. Oh, and I heard Amber's boyfriend pull up at her caravan - they're not supposed to park on the grass,' he grouched.

I open my mouth to ask more questions, but Jim turns abruptly and whistles at Rusty. 'Come on, boy, you'll be thirsty and I'm starving!'

It's obvious that he won't talk anymore because he storms off down the side of the caravan and enters their door.

Celia shrugs her shoulders and leans towards me in a secretive manner. She whispers, 'Sorry, Clive, that was rude of him, but he's not himself lately and I'm worried. He's behaving very strangely and is up through the night with nightmares where he shouts and rambles words that I can't understand then paces about the caravan,' she says wrinkling her brow. 'But he won't see the doctor because he's frightened. He looks dreadful and isn't eating properly so he's losing weight. It's almost as though he's haunted by something.'

I nod. 'Well, I've only just met you both, but I agree he doesn't seem as happy as he did when I first came for tea.'

Her eyes fill with tears, and I pray she isn't going to cry. I could only just cope with Liz crying, but Celia is a different woman altogether. Liz is outspoken and loud. She lets her feelings out without concern of losing control. If Celia broke down, it would be far worse because she's very proud and would see it as an embarrassment.

She croaks, 'He used to be quick at picking things up, but I can tell he can't seem to organise his thoughts to give a proper answer? And I can't keep his attention for long either.'

We are both startled when Jim shouts through to her, 'Celia, please come inside and cook lunch!' She waves goodbye then scuttles inside her veranda doors and I wander back to my chair.

I slump back down in front of the laptop. My stomach is churning with the two snippets of information from Jim and decide to note them down in case I need them as evidence at a later date.

I could tell when Jim mentioned how I was questioning people that I've made him uncomfortable which was never my intention. I wouldn't want to make anyone feel like this, but I didn't have that effect on Celia, therefore, I wonder if Jim does have something to hide? I reckon he knows more than he's letting on and sigh heavily. I do hope he's not involved with Audrey's death because they both seem such nice people. A little voice nags in the back of my mind saying, not so nice if he can push an old lady to the ground and dump her in the sea.

Reading Jim's body language, it is easy to spot the signs of a guilty conscience – heavens, I write them often enough. The avoidance of eye contact, the shuffling of his feet, the snappiness with Celia about getting the night mixed up, the tugging of his ear and puffing hard on his vape. However, I suppose these signs could be just down to worry about his ill-health which talking to Celia afterwards is a major concern to them both.

In Jim's desperate state of mind, could he have done this? Maybe he just snapped and knocked Audrey to the ground? And, I reckon, he would be strong enough to carry Audrey to the causeway or maybe put the old lady in his car and dump her?

But there again, if Jim did have memory loss could he have forgotten all about it? He may have no recollection of that night after he'd walked Rusty. Which begs the next question –

what would he have done with Rusty if this had happened? Surely, someone would have heard the dog barking as he carried Audrey to his car? And, even if his memory is coming and going our minds have the ability to block out horrible events.

These observations fit in with what I learnt online about early onset Alzheimer's. However, the mix up of Monday and Tuesday could simply be that Jim switched off from Celia's ranting - like he's already admitted to doing.

I now think about Amber. She told me that Kieran had arrived on Tuesday at 9pm, but not according to Jim who said he pulled up on the grass well after midnight on Monday. So, who is telling the truth? And, if Jim is correct then why would Amber lie? Possibly to give Kieran an alibi? I rub my chin with so many questions but no answers.

Chapter Twenty Nine

I'm wondering whether to call and see Amber the next morning to clarify exactly what day and time Kieran arrived, but as I walk down the path towards her caravan, I see the back of their car heading up the road. The gigglers are waving and pulling faces at me through the back window. I figure they're maybe having a day out away from the park and decide to do the same myself. Or at least the morning off from writing because I wrote well into last night. Which is unusual for me, but the progress I've made with Jason in Durham spurs me on, and I have a spring in my step when I walk past the lodge.

Maud and Liz are in the garden sitting on old deck chairs in the sun and they call me over. I walk through the gate and greet them both warmly.

Liz opens up another chair and Maud says, 'Take the weight off your feet a moment and have a glass of lemonade - I made it this morning.'

I sit down on the chair. Who still makes lemonade these days when it's so easy to buy a bottle, I think and take a gulp of the long, cold drink. My shoulders droop and my mouth tingles with the refreshing lemony flavour. 'Oh, my days, that's absolutely lovely.'

Maud raises her chin and nods in satisfaction.

'Actually, I was going to ring you, Liz, to say that the police haven't spoken to the night-shift security officer.'

I tell them about my evening visit to see him and how there wasn't anything to report. Maud tuts loudly and Liz shakes her head.

However, they both look better than the last time I saw them, especially Liz. She has her layers of thick make-up back in place that I haven't seen for a few days which makes her look more like her usual self.

'We've been to see Mam in the funeral parlour this morning,' Liz says. 'And, the one thing I can say is that she looks a lot more peaceful than the last time I saw her down in the sea.'

I nod and give her my best sympathetic smile. 'And that's the best way to remember her. I know this has got to be so difficult for you both - it would be hard enough coping with Audrey dying but, in these circumstances…' I say and gulp at the lemonade. 'Well, my heart goes out to you both.'

Maud is wearing old-fashioned black sunglasses so I can't see her eyes, but Liz's are wet, and she nods. 'It is, Clive, although it was good to see Mam even though there's no date to release her body for burial as yet.'

Maud smooths down her blue checky skirt and smiles at me. 'Yes, and we've finalised the details for the funeral,' she says. 'I want my sister to have the best because the end of her life has been so traumatic.'

Liz nods. 'We've decided that Mam will be taken in the hearse from here at our lodge gate and driven around the park so all the staff can pay their respects. The hearse will weave up and down the smaller paths amongst all the caravans, come back out onto the main road and along to the cemetery. '

I nod and drain the lemonade. 'That's a great idea so Audrey will see the whole park that she's built up over the years for the last time. I bet she knew each section like the back of her hand?'

Liz smiles and lifts her chin. 'Of course, she did, just like I do. When you design and build areas on a plot for expansion it becomes personal. I remember every year that we made changes and have photos of the excavations that took place.'

I watch Liz jump up and hurry inside. I figure she is going to get photographs and although I won't have a great deal of interest in them, I know it's important to Liz.

Maud leans across and pats the back of my hand. 'Elizabeth is getting a little better each day and isn't as distraught as she was on Monday,' she says. 'And since I arrived, I think she's sleeping more because I haven't heard her get up through the night as she had been doing.'

I nod. 'That's good to hear because she was in a terrible state on Sunday and Monday. I suppose it just takes time.'

Maud removes her glasses as the sun goes behind a cloud and nods. 'Yes, as the old saying goes, time is a great healer.'

I can see her eyes now and they do seem a little puffy, but she's not upset.

'And,' I say. 'I'm sure you being here has been a great help.'

Liz returns with a big photo album. It has a green cover with The Mathews Caravan Park on the front. Liz drags her chair next to mine and places it on my knee to describes all of the different photos.

As predicted, I'm not particularly interested in the building shots, but it's amazing to see Liz and Audrey in their younger days. Liz was a stunning young woman in her thirties wearing white shorty-shorts which didn't leave much to anyone's imagination. And Audrey looked smart in a flowery pink dress where she must have been in her sixties. The photo has been taken in the Entertainment Centre with a poster of Tom Jones in the background. By their clothes and lifestyle, I can tell they've always been quite well-to-do.

'Hey,' I say and grin. 'Look at you two living the high life with the celebrities!'

Now I see mother and daughter in a different light and, in their heyday. They look a formidable team together - on top of their game and definitely going places. The great reputation and respect they have from people in the community nowadays began here years ago. I whistle in awe.

Liz smiles and traces a finger down a close-up shot of Audrey's face. 'We did,' she says. 'Of course, this was long before her memory began to fade, and that horrible Alzheimer's took over.'

An old photograph on a card is tucked in the back of the album and Liz holds it almost reverentially in her hand. The photo is of a young soldier, and I stare over her shoulder at his uniform. It looks familiar to me which is strange because my knowledge of the army could fit onto a postage stamp. But I know I've seen it lately somewhere.

'Who's this? An uncle?' I ask. 'He looks very young to be in a uniform, doesn't he?'

Liz takes a deep breath and tells me how she's just discovered the photograph and has learned that Audrey had a baby boy adopted when she was sixteen.

I see Maud's shoulders stiffen and her face flush. 'Really, Elizabeth, there's no need to be telling everyone about this.'

Liz shakes her head. 'First, Aunt Maud, Clive isn't just anybody, and second of all, there's no reason to keep this a family secret,' she says. 'Mam's no longer here to be embarrassed about it and to be honest nobody these days thinks of single mothers as a disgrace.'

Phew, I think, Liz has certainly been through the wringer. Not only is she grieving for Audrey after a horrible death, but now she finds out that she has a half-brother. Sometimes life knows how to deal out the blows, I reckon and touch her shoulder. 'Of course, they don't,' I say. 'And

I'm remembering the old saying, Audrey wasn't the first and certainly won't be the last.'

'This is a soldier who Mam had a love affair with when she worked at Seaton Delaval Hall,' she says. 'Apparently, he didn't even know she was pregnant when he returned home to Germany.'

'That's it!' I cry. 'That's where I saw the uniform up at the hall on old photographs.'

Liz nods. 'Then poor Mam was packed off to Carlisle into a home for wayward girls where she had the baby and had to stay working for her keep until she was eighteen.'

I whistle between my teeth with amazement at this story. It makes me think of the film, Philomena with Judy Dench playing the lead character. 'God, life was so cruel back then,' I say and glance at Maud who has lowered her head. She doesn't look up at us and fiddles with a white ribbon at the neck of her blouse.

Maud mumbles, 'You're right there, Clive. Life was hard and cruel, but we just did our best to get through it all – we had no other choice.'

Looking up I see Maud's damp eyes. Liz gets up, goes to her aunt, and squeezes her shoulder. 'I'm not getting at you because I know what you did was for Mam's own good – it's just very hard to understand in this day and age.'

It's obvious the two of them have had earlier words about the situation. However, I can see a certain bond between them now which wasn't there the day she arrived in a tense atmosphere.

Perhaps Mary Poppins had mellowed after her spit-spot inspection and was showing her softer side? She was bound to be grieving for her only sister and maybe this had brought her and Liz together a little more. I smile, whatever's brought this about I know Audrey would be pleased to see the new relationship between niece and aunt.

I say, 'Liz, if you need help to trace your half-brother then just shout up. I don't know a great deal about tracing relatives and adoption, but as they say, two heads are better than one.'

Liz smiles. 'Thanks, Clive, but I'm not sure if that's something I want to know about just yet – maybe one day but not at the moment.'

I see Maud take a big sigh of what I take as relief. She smiles at Liz and takes her hand. 'I don't expect you young ones to even imagine what it was like in the 1940s, but as the oldest sister Audrey was my responsibility.'

I nod encouragingly at her while my mind whirls. Did the person who knocked Audrey to the ground have something to do with this even though it was over seventy years ago? I sigh, stranger things have occurred, I suppose.

Liz returns to her seat and lights a cigarette.

Maud sits forward. 'The one thing that is niggling in the back of my mind is the fact that Audrey was found on the side steps to the causeway because that's where she used to meet her soldier…' she says and stares down at her hand twirling around her wedding ring. Pursing her lips she continues, 'And that's where the shenanigans took place. Although, I must say in her defence, Audrey did love him.'

The previous sad look descends upon Liz's face again and her eyes fill with tears. Probably the mention of the causeway has brought Audrey's image back to her mind because it has done with me too. I still see her bloated face and tangled hair with seaweed when I think of Audrey.

Liz cries, 'I mean, who would do such a thing to a little old lady? Mam was in her nightdress, for goodness sake,' she says. 'I feel so angry about what happened to her and know that someone has to pay for doing this, Clive. She was my mam and has been chucked in the sea like a piece of bloody rubbish!'

Maud folds her arms across her chest and bristles. 'Oh, they will, Elizabeth,' she snaps back. 'Don't worry because we'll find out what happened supposing it's the last thing I do!'

And I believe her. I guess when you reach ninety-two, you end up with a devil-may-care attitude to life. And Maud is bound to want to get to the bottom of what happened to her sister.

I try to distract Liz from getting more upset and ask, 'Is there anyone on the park that you think is a little dodgy? Or as they say on TV programs, do you know of anyone that would want to harm Audrey?'

I can see Liz is thinking hard and I ask, 'Maybe a dissatisfied customer? Or someone refusing to pay a bill?' I say. 'Have you had a run-in with anyone?'

She draws on her cigarette and furrows her eyebrows. 'The only person that I thought was a bit weird was a youngish man who checked-in the day before you, but I can't remember his name without looking in the diary,' she says. 'At first, I'd thought, oh, he's a big, chunky guy and I might be onto a winner because he kept staring at me.'

I imagine Liz giving him the hungry-eye as she had done with me when I'd checked-in at the desk.

Maud clicks her tongue in annoyance and shakes her head, 'Really, Elizabeth!'

My curiosity is piqued. 'So, what happened then?'

Liz shakes her head at Maud and continues, 'I decided he was a bit creepy because he strode over and stared through the snug door at Mam. He was looking her up and down and it unsettled Mam - she began to cry. So, I hurried through his check-in details, got him out of reception and went to soothe her.'

Liz looks over my shoulder as though she is still thinking about the incident. 'And then Mam said the strangest thing - she kept whispering the same words, dark brown eyes. Oooh, those brown eyes and came over all dreamy. I remember thinking it was as if Mam knew him but of course she didn't.'

Maud tuts again, 'I think this is being rather fanciful, Elizabeth, the man probably just reminded her of someone, that's all.'

I sit back in my chair deep in thought. And of course, Maud could be right, and this guy looked like someone Audrey once knew. Is there a chance that Liz is right and there was something weird about him? It's not normal for a youngish man to stare at an old woman. Often younger people don't know how to manage conversations with the confused and elderly. Of course, there are exceptions to this, but as a rule an ordinary man would shy away from a rambling old woman. But he hadn't.

'Actually, 'Liz says. 'He's staying in the caravan behind you.'

It's Dennis, aka Slack-Jowls, I think, and cry, 'Oh, I've met him!'

Chapter Thirty

I leave the ladies and walk out onto the main road. I hop onto a bus and alight in the opposite direction at Seaton Sluice. The pamphlet I have from reception tells me, the village sits at the southern end of a glimmering expanse of golden sand in a three mile, dune-backed band to Blyth. I find the little harbour area charming and stop to read the information board where I learn that it had been famous for salt pans.

In the 1600s Sir Ralph Delaval had a pier constructed and then Sir John Hussey Delaval had a new entrance made for the harbour by blasting a channel through solid rock, providing what was known as, The Cut. I remember all I'd learned about the family at the hall and know the Delaval's have made a big difference to the area.

I have to admit they did a good job, and the transformation was something that not only helped their business and coffers but also the local community. Apparently, there had been a huge bottle-works here until it was demolished to make way for new houses.

I look around the houses and wonder where Maud and Audrey had lived and try to imagine what the little harbour area looked like when they were sixteen and eighteen. The poverty and poor conditions they lived in must have been a daily struggle. Let alone walking to the hall every day to work. They wouldn't have been able to hop onto a bus like we all can now.

I remember my visit to the hall and the German POWs in the East Wing and sigh. I know Audrey really loved him and wondered when he was lying in his bunk at night if he felt the same for her. I frown thinking of poor Audrey, being single, pregnant and alone must have been terrifying. I could tell the way Maud had hung her head and spoken in a defensive manner that she felt like the big bad wolf in what had happened.

Also, it was obvious that Liz and Maud had had heated words about the adoption in Carlisle. But who are we to judge - we weren't trying to survive in the 1940s. Plus a young woman's life must have been so different to a man's.

I read how the word, Seaton is an old English meaning for a settlement by the sea. I look around and can tell it fits the name because that's exactly what it is although the information says there are now approximately 3,000 people live here. Small boats are moored in the harbour which is surrounded by grassy banks, and I take a quick photo to send to Barbie - she'll love the natural landscape.

With my stomach growling I head into The King's Arms for lunch. It's a large pub and restaurant which is painted white and takes centre stage in the harbour area. Outside are tables and chairs with sailors rope threaded in between huge old beer barrels forming the edges of the paved area.

It looks well-kept and I lick my lips reading the menu outside. Once inside I sit at a wood table on a green padded chair. There are a few couples already eating and I glance across at their meals to see the plates piled with mince and dumplings. That's for me, I think and order straight away with an orange juice.

The beef mince and onions in a rich gravy is tasty and I know Barbie would be pleased to see I'm eating the first choice of vegetables since I left home. With a full belly now, I wander around the outside of, The Octagon, which is a small castellated building. It was built as the Harbour Office but is now a private art gallery. I marvel at the old stone and turrets around the top then whistling I begin to walk back down to the caravan park.

I can't help thinking about what Liz told me this morning as I near the park. It's impossible to imagine how I'd feel if I suddenly found out that I had a half-sibling who I knew nothing about. Indeed, it had been enough of a shock discovering my grandfather existed last year.

Growing up over the years, I'd often wished for a sibling so I wouldn't be on my own with the parents. Now, as an adult, I know this wouldn't have been the right reason to have a brother or sister. Unlike other people, I have no longing for the familiarity of home. Others, like Barbie, have childhood memories of beloved houses, their own bedrooms, cosy kitchen areas and family mealtimes around a big table – I never had this.

I've not once been back to Doncaster and the rooms where I'd spent my days feeling scared. The images of drug-fuelled fights in the lounge and kitchen flash briefly into my mind and I know the memories will never leave me – they're too grotesque. In fact, I would struggle now to remember where the house was, even though Barbie has offered to come with me and put the ghosts to rest. But I simply couldn't.

So, I shrug, although I wouldn't have wished the awful side of my childhood on anybody it would have been good now as an adult to share nice things with someone.

I know if I was Liz, I'd definitely want to trace this half-brother who was adopted. However, I also know how much she's been through lately and it's perfectly understandable if she doesn't want more upheaval in her life. I smile, perhaps when Maud returns to Devon after the funeral and she's alone with time to think properly she may want to trace him. For her sake, I hope she does.

***

I turn onto the path for Ash Mews and up ahead I see Slack-Jowls, aka, Dennis, talking to Amber outside her caravan. It's obvious that the family are back from their outing, although the car is missing and there's no sign of Kieran. I can hear the girls on the veranda playing and giggling.

'Hey, there,' I say approaching them both. 'It's another fine day.'

Dennis makes a point of stretching his hand out and I take it in mine. I wince before he grasps my hand expecting the pain this time. I manage to smile at him, but inside I'm berating myself for being such a wimp. It's time to man-up, I think.

'Hi, Clive,' Amber says but doesn't look directly at me. She seems to avoid eye contact much as Jim had done and I'm beginning to get a little paranoid about their reactions. Mostly, people who do this are what I'd call, shifty, with something significant to hide. But do these two have something they don't want to tell me? I'm not sure.

As the car is gone, I ask, 'So, where's Kieran?'

Amber looks at me with her huge brown eyes which now have dark circles underneath. The cream coloured T-Shirt she is wearing seems to make them look even bigger.

'Oh, he's gone off to a big job with loads of money which is great for him,' she mumbles. 'Not that I see any of it.'

I wonder again why this beautiful woman puts up with the toss-pot but know it's none of my business. 'Ahh,' I mutter and tell them about my great lunch.

'I'll have to try that restaurant,' Dennis says. 'It sounds very good.'

I remember what Liz had told me about Dennis checking into reception and how he'd stared at both Liz and Audrey. What kind of a man stares at an old lady? I look at him again now but in a different light.

Dennis is sturdy and strong that's for sure. He looks like he can handle himself if needed and a small voice in the back of my mind says an old lady would be very easy for him to carry. He has a self-assured look about him and I'd noticed on the day of the search for Audrey how he'd strutted rather than walked with his shoulders pulled back.

Dennis says, 'It's such tragic news about the old lady dead on the causeway, is it not?'

I swallow hard and nod. 'Yeah, it's awful,' I say. 'I'm only praying that the police can find whoever is responsible for doing this.'

Amber launches into the tale about how they'd found Audrey and I notice Dennis knit his bushy eyebrows together as he concentrates hard listening to her words. His brown eyes are hooded, and his blond hair is thin in places. I've decided he is definitely older than me and would say late thirties. However, I suppose he could be younger if he'd had a hard life which has aged him.

I look down to his old sandals and notice he's taken off his socks today. I see his toes wriggle when he speaks – a sign of nerves, I wonder?

He tells us both how he's been over to the lighthouse and was fascinated about the heritage with being a history buff.

It's the word, buff that makes me think again about his strange accent. It's bugged me since the first time I spoke to him because I can't decide where it's from. Most accents I can guess at especially, Scottish, Irish, and Welsh or even stronger twangs like Liverpool scouse or London cockney but this has me stumped. And, it was the way he'd asked, 'Is it not?'

This sounds to me as though he has learned English from a dictionary because I'm convinced now that it's not his first language. And although his pronunciation is very good it sounds stilted.

A loud wail comes from behind us and Amber groans at the noise of the girls quarrelling. 'Sorry, guys,' she says. 'I'll have to go.'

She turns and sashays down the path in her tight skinny jeans. I take a side-glance at Dennis to see his eyes fixed and staring at her bottom. Yep, I can see how those intense hooded eyes staring at someone would make them uncomfortable and frighten an old lady. I turn away from Dennis and he drags his eyes away from Amber then mumbles goodbye.

While I walk away, I notice for the first time how the blinds on his caravan windows are open and remember what Jim had told me about Monday night. Unlocking my caravan door, I wonder if Slack-Jowls did have something to do with Audrey's demise? But there again, during their conversation he was the one who brought up the subject of Audrey's death and if you did have something to hide, you'd hardly draw attention to the matter, would you?

While I switch on the kettle and lift open the lid on my laptop I remember the Soham murderer, Ian Huntley. He'd been a caretaker at the girls' school and had loved the limelight, TV camera crew, and giving many interviews. Which, I reckon is another way of drawing attention to oneself.

Chapter Thirty One
Dennis Muller

Dennis flopped down onto the sofa in his caravan and chewed the side of his moustache. That was a close call, he thought and knew he had to be more careful. If he wasn't, the interfering author, Clive, would put two and two together and he'd be found out. Which was the last thing he wanted at this stage. He had to find out more about his other family.

He looked at the photograph in a frame of his fiancé, Lena, and smiled. He missed her more than he thought possible since he'd left home last week. They had been separated for work trips on many occasions when he had flown around Europe, but this time it seemed different somehow. He'd made this a road trip driving across France and over on the ferry to England. In the past, he had been to London a few times but never to the North East. This was a different place altogether.

The frame wasn't quite straight on the unit, and he jumped up to set it level on the wood shelf. Dennis couldn't bear things that were out of kilter – everything had to be correct and in its rightful place.

The photograph had been taken when they were on top of Wank Mountain which is the back drop to their town, Garmisch-Partenkirchen, the highest ski area in Germany. The grey, three-pointed mountain loomed behind all of the houses and train station in the town being seen from every angle. Lena was grinning into the camera when he'd taken the photograph last year – it had been the day he proposed and slipped the simple but expensive ring onto her finger.

Dennis imagined Lena in the kitchen at home now throwing a dish of his favourite sauerkraut together with cabbage, berries, and a strong yellow mustard. He licked his lips almost drooling at the thought and smell.

They'd bought a house in the town centre because neither him nor Lena would ever want to live elsewhere. Or at least that's what they told each other. Bavaria was home to both their families, and they knew nothing else. Lena's parents and family lived to the left of their new house and his own parents, Colin and Greta lived in a bigger house to their right.

Dennis looked out of the window of the caravan and could just see the tip of the lighthouse in the distance. He was slightly jealous of Clive having the close-up, spectacular view over to the lighthouse. There again, he hadn't paid extra for his caravan as Clive would have done.

There was something about Clive that got under his skin. He was, what women would call, a good-looking man. He was pleasant, chatty and friendly. However, there was a look in his eyes that Dennis had seen twice now upon meeting him. This had made the hairs on the back of his neck bristle. It was as though Clive could see inside him. He knew the signs of a suspicious mind and Clive certainly had one. Dennis shrugged – maybe it was because he wrote about crime and liked mysterious circumstances? He wasn't sure but knew he had to take care around him.

Dennis picked at the dry skin on his lip and thought of his earlier walk along the seafront by the cemetery. The houses here were totally different to their homes in Bavaria. They all looked the same in red bricks with PVC windows. Whereas his house and all of the others in Garmish, were highly decorated with paintings and drawings on the outside walls. Lena has chosen three different traditional folk tales to have painted by an artist next month in cream, green, and rich pink colours on theirs.

Dennis knew the weather here was not conducive to outside decoration. Garmish had its fair share of rain usually in one swift downpour in an afternoon and then sunshine for the rest of the day.

Since he was a young boy his grandfather, Sebastian had sat him on his knee to tell him stories of his time in England during the war. Dennis had fond memories of his grandfather's crinkly-leather lederhosen and hairy knees. They weren't often worn nowadays unless people worked in the tourist industry and shops, but Dennis remembered the lederhosen with affection.

As he'd grown older, Dennis had badgered him into more tales because he was fascinated in their family tree - obsessional some might say. He wanted to know all about his ancestry although his father wasn't interested whatsoever. Completing his DNA on big websites and databases was relatively easy and had thrown up matches in England, namely, the North East.

Sebastian told him how he'd fallen in love with the young girl, Audrey and how he had spent his time in the POW billet in Seaton Delaval Hall. The stories of their passion and the love they'd made after strolling along the beach in the darkness of night with only the stars above them. And then on the causeway over to the lighthouse which Sebastian had felt was standing guard over their secret rendezvous. Dennis still missed his grandfather even though he'd long since died. Sebastian had been a huge influence in his life and a man with a big heart.

Feeling the Velcro strap on his sandal wasn't quite right, he leaned over and tightened it. Although the sandals weren't new, they appeared slacker than usual, and Dennis fretted – was he losing weight? Lena had thought so last month but he'd lied and flatly denied the claim. Considering he hadn't weighed himself, Dennis felt his cheeks flush. He didn't usually tell lies to Lena or anyone else for that matter. He had always thought of himself as honest and an honourable man.

Dennis got up and began to pace around the caravan feeling restless. He looked out of the side window at the back of the caravan and down towards the bottom of the park with its main driveway. This view brought back memories of the first time he saw Liz and Audrey in their reception.

Audrey, of course, didn't have the same dark brown eyes that he and Sebastian had but he recognised the similar shaping in her face and nose – there'd been a definite family resemblance to him. He'd gasped in shock, and it had taken every inch of his composure not to cry out aloud. This similarity, Dennis reckoned was the reason why he had behaved out of character and appeared rude to the ladies.

He had left reception with the caravan key and felt bad because he'd obviously upset the old lady by staring at her. He hadn't been able to stop himself. After all the years of wondering about the other side of his family tree, he had been right there, standing in front of his grandmother and aunt. It had blown his mind a little and flung him into a spin.

Now, he thought of Sebastian and knew his grandfather wouldn't be proud of him for behaving in such a manner. It wasn't the Bavarian way and he had been raised with better standards of etiquette. He shrugged, it was done now and there was no going back. If he'd had the time again, he would have behaved with more respect for his elders.

Dennis hadn't wanted to launch straight in with the words, 'Hey there, I'm your grandson!' He was biding his time.

He had watched them in the lodge from a distance for the first few days mainly at night because he didn't want to be recognised. He'd also invented the migraine excuse to keep his blinds drawn throughout the day so people couldn't see what he was doing.

Jotting down their movements had formed a pattern between the lodge and reception. Dennis wanted to be prepared and ready to meet them properly. He wanted to be rehearsed in his words and thoughts for the conversation. He didn't want to mess it up.

His stomach rumbled. Dennis missed their German food especially the white asparagus which would be in season and amazing sausages. Although he had to admit, the fish and chips on the seafront were very good and decided to wander down to eat. He pulled on his jacket and picked up his kindle to read in the cafe. He loved thrillers and was enjoying the latest novel by Clive Thompson. Not that he'd told him this. Dennis didn't want to be on a friendly relationship with Clive because he didn't trust him.

With the key in his hand, Dennis began his security checks to leave. TV switched off at the plug. All lights were off. Blinds closed but not fully. And then he sighed remembering he hadn't washed his hands.

He hurried into the bathroom and turned on the hot water tap. He let it run for a while until steam was rising and opened the overhead cabinet. There were five bars of soap to choose from and he grabbed the one that had been used the least. This was from Friday, he reckoned and knew any bugs would have disappeared by now. Lathering his hands, he took a steel nail brush and scrubbed all areas of his hands. He winced at the hot water but persevered knowing he was purging himself of bacteria and germs.

Leaving the caravan, he locked the door and tried the handle three times. Yep, he thought, definitely locked and all was safe. He wouldn't want anyone to see inside at the moment. Dennis walked down the ramp and stood still rubbing his jaw. Had he locked the door? Often, he tried to fight the repetitive actions, but didn't have the energy today, so scurried back to the door and tried the handle once more to quell his agitation.

Heading down to the main road, Dennis thought of how he had loved his grandfather and mother who were true Bavarian. But, as they say in England, his father was a different kettle of fish altogether.

Dennis knew his mission was near completion and sighed. He'd come all this way to see and meet his grandmother but had never got the chance to talk to her. He grimaced, there was only his aunt Elizabeth left now.

Chapter Thirty Two

I've written all day and reckon my last chapter only has one more scene to finalise, so I'm well-chuffed with my progress. I am longing to write the words, The End. Not far from doing this, I write the phrase, 'He had a steely jaw of determination.'

I smile. A little like myself, I think when there's a tap at the caravan door. Although, I'm on the veranda I jump up and head down the ramp to see Liz standing wringing her hands.

She's wearing a pretty, lemon sundress and I smile with pleasure to see her look a little more feminine. It makes a nice change to her casual jeans and low-cut tops.

'Hey,' I call walking towards her. 'What's up?'

'Oh, there's nothing wrong,' she says smoothing the dress down over her thighs. 'I just wondered if I could take you up on the offer to help me start tracing my brother. I don't want to talk about this in front of Aunt Maud.'

I smile and nod. 'Of course, I will, although I'm not sure how much help I can actually be, but I'll give it a whirl.' I turn and wave my hand. 'I'm on the veranda with my laptop – come and sit with me.'

She follows me onto the veranda and looks out to sea. 'Oh, I forgotten what a lovely view this is – we've got the main road out the back of our garden,' she says. 'Mam built our lodge when I was still at school, but I think I would have chosen a different position and view if I'd had a say in the matter.'

I stand next to her at the railing. 'Audrey probably wanted to be as close to reception as possible?'

She nods and spins around looking through the doors to the inside of the caravan. I follow her gaze and see my clothes slung over the back of the sofa, dishes in the sink, papers and my notes spread over the coffee table. I feel like I'm on inspection and make a move to hurry inside and tidy them away. 'Sorry about the mess,' I mutter.

Liz shakes her head. 'Oh, please don't – it's fine,' she says.

And with a twinkle in her eye, I haven't seen for a while, she says, 'I wouldn't expect anything else from a man on his own.'

I give her a sheepish nod and sit down in front of my laptop while she pulls over another chair next to mine.

I glance from the corner of my eye while closing down my document and say, 'Pretty dress…'

She gives a throaty laugh. 'Yeah, well, it's Sunday so me and aunt Maud have been to church and I figured it would be worth making the effort to keep the peace.'

I nod opening Google and look at her. 'I get the impression that relations between you are on the up? And, for what it's worth, I don't think she

suits the Mary Poppins send-up because I like
her.'

Looking back at the screen, I say, 'She's just a
fussy old lady with plenty of gusto – look at the
way she tackled Ted Barker our friendly police
inspector.'

Liz throws her head back and laughs. 'Oh,
yeah, she's plenty of gusto alright,' she says.
'But, on a more serious note, you're right. We
are getting along better than we ever have and to
be honest, I would have hated going through all
of this on my own.'

I nod and concentrate. 'Right, so where do we
start? I mean, I'm not sure I can do any more
than you could do at home on your own? But as
I said before, sometimes two heads are than
one.'

Liz looks at the screen. 'Well, all I've done so
far is watch the TV show, DNA Family Secrets,
where there was a man looking for his sister
who'd been adopted - the manager of genetics
said he would only have a quarter of DNA to
work with.'

Hmm. I think, if nothing else this is going to be
interesting. I type into the search box, how to
trace adopted relatives, and we both begin to
look at the posts that appear on the screen. We
trawl through a few reading the notes and find
an array of information which apparently is also
available from The General Register Office.

Liz reaches into her shoulder bag and pulls out
a little notebook and pen. 'I'll just scribble down

the main headings in case I need to look at them again.'

I open another search box and type in, adoption records. This gives us many more articles but mainly for people who are adopted and want to trace their parents on the government website.

'Not that helpful,' I say. 'You're the other way around and searching from the mother's viewpoint, so this isn't much good.'

We find Adoption Services Agency who would look for her brother's birth certificate, but we don't have this detail and I frown. 'It's such a shame that we don't have his birth date because we'd be able to get much further.'

As a last ditch effort, I look at a site called Ancestry where apparently we can get parents' names, ages, jobs, and residence with birthplaces for both child, parents and religious denomination. It claims to be the largest online.

'I know,' Liz says and jots down the agency name. 'But if I get more information then these people might be able to trace him.'

I shrug while Liz pulls out her sunglasses, puts them on and leans back in the chair listening. Conscious of Amber and Celia on either sides of my caravan, and the fact that Liz might not want them to know her business, I read out the following information in a quiet voice. 'Initially adoptions in the UK were closed, meaning the adoptee's birth records and previous name and family history were sealed. Often the child was not told they were adopted and would only find out at a later stage of their life. This could be difficult and distressing for everyone involved. But a new birth certificate is now produced in the child's adoptive name. This document is known as an adoption certificate and replaces the original birth certificate for all legal purposes.'

In another article, she sits forward, and we both read, 'During WWII, The Society saw a record number of adoptions. Unfortunately, once American soldiers passed away fighting in the war, their wives were unable to support their children, leaving no choice but to put their children up for adoption. Father dead, mother unable to support five children.'

Liz clicks her tongue. 'Well, Aunt Maud says she can't remember the name of the nursing home in Carlisle – it's too long ago,' she says. 'And at first I'd thought she was simply being awkward, but now I don't think so because I think she'd like to help.'

I nod. 'Yes, I think she would, too,' I say and type into the search box, nursing homes in Carlisle 1949. It pings up with a few posts all naming the same one. 'Well, there only seems to be one from back then so that does narrows things down somewhat.'

Liz leans over my shoulder and I get a slight whiff of a musk perfume. We read at the same time the nursing home statement. 'The object of the home was the reclamation of 'fallen girls' from the servant class and training them to be able to earn their own living. The home could house up to thirty girls aged from seventeen to thirty-five years old. They were expected to remain for two years. Those from outside the area and diocese were required to pay £5. In 1892, the work was part of an income to support the running of the home. In 1926, the home moved to new premises where the girls were then called, 'friendless and fallen.'

I take a sideways look at Liz and her faces flushes bright red. I can tell she is outraged and begins to rant, 'How dare they! Fallen and friendless? My mam was neither of these – she had Maud and her friends. And, where on God's earth does the word, fallen come into anything - bloody cruelty – that's what it was!'

She curses more and wrings her hands together then jumps up and begins to pace back and forth along the veranda. I cringe at her choice swear words and can practically see the air turn blue. I only hope it's not loud enough to disturb Celia and the gigglers next door. I sit back patiently letting her run out of steam.

'Liz, calm yourself,' I say. 'It was just the done thing back then. Single mothers were pressurised to give up their babies because to have children out of wedlock was a social stigma.'

Liz stops pacing and slumps down into the chair again. She seems to deflate like a balloon, but I can see her eyes are watery. I pray she isn't going to cry.

She sniffles and pulls out her packet of cigarettes. 'My mam wasn't a s…stigma! She worked hard all of her life after that one slip-up,' she says. 'And at sixteen she was little more than a child herself.'

'I totally agree, but we can't change history – mores the pity,' I say. 'And all of her customers, friends, family, and especially you, know different, which is the main thing so don't upset yourself, eh?'

Liz lights her cigarette and I see her taking deep breaths slowly in and out. She says, 'You taught me this breathing technique down at the causeway and I use it now when I get agitated which at the moment seems to be a regular occurrence.'

'That's good and more than understandable because you've so much to cope with,' I say. 'I know I must sound like a parrot repeating myself but just try to take one day at a time.'

I can see she is calming herself and offer, 'Look, it says to contact them if you have any enquiries. But because it's Sunday and office staff won't be at work – why not take the number and try to ring tomorrow?'

She picks up her pen and I see her hands trembling as she jots down the number.

'I will,' she states. 'And if I don't get any information from them, I'll take the train to Carlisle and go myself to sort it out.'

I can tell she's got the bit between her teeth now and her determination will override the upset. I want to say, that's my girl, but think differently. It's something I would say to Barbie, but know Liz is a totally different woman.

'Well, I'd better get back to Aunt Maud,' she says. 'Thanks, Clive for helping with this and I'll let you know what they say.'

She stands up and smooths down her dress then walks along the ramp. I follow her and just before we say good bye I notice a twitching of the blinds at the caravan where Dennis is staying. Has he been watching us? Although he wouldn't be able to see us on the veranda from the front of his caravan.

My suspicious mind kicks-in. 'Liz, I know when I filled in the forms to come here, I had to input my home address. So, can you remember where Dennis is from? Is there an address on your computer?'

She pauses and shakes her head. 'Nope, but I'll have a look when I get back,' she says and whispers. 'Why? Have you found out something about him? I still think he's a little strange.'

I shake my head. 'Not yet, but let's just say, I'm working on a hunch.'

Liz leaves and I head back inside and make a coffee. I tut at the used cups in the sink, shrug and take out another clean mug. I promise myself that as soon as I finish my chapter, I'll tidy-up. Sitting back outside, I sip the coffee and dunk in two jammy-dodger biscuits when my mobile tinkles.

I look down and read a text from Liz. 'Dennis's address is in, Garmish, Bavaria.'

Yes, I whoop and dance a jig! Here's my first genuine lead.

Chapter Thirty Three

Maud

Maud woke up from dozing on the couch and cried, 'It was April Fool's Day!'

She shook herself awake remembering how Elizabeth had gone out for a walk. Maud raised an eyebrow, or that's what her niece had said. However, she knew Elizabeth had gone to see Clive about the adoption in Carlisle. After all, he had offered to help. Maud smirked - she might be old, but she wasn't daft - well, not yet anyway.

Maud had spent the day wracking her brain trying to remember something, anything about Carlisle and Audrey's stay. She'd never thought she would hear herself say this, but now the secret was out in the open, she desperately wanted to help. However, it was so long ago.

When she was trying to remember she couldn't, but when she was asleep it had flashed back into her mind. How did that work? Maybe a sign at nearly ninety two, she was following in her sister's footsteps and her brain wasn't as sharp as it always had been.

She got up and strode into the kitchen to make a fresh cup of tea. Whilst boiling the kettle she picked up a notebook from the dresser and began to write down everything she could remember from her sleep, or had it been a dream? She hoped, no prayed, it wasn't a fanciful dream because if she told Elizabeth and it wasn't right, it would cause more upset which was the last thing she wanted.

They'd seemed to find a new path between themselves since the day she'd arrived, and Maud didn't want to lose this. In the past, Maud knew that her niece thought she was a ridiculous old woman and had once overheard Elizabeth calling her Mary Poppins. She had shrugged it off at the time knowing the name calling could have been worse. It was just that she liked things done properly which was the total opposite to Audrey's slap-happy way. However, she could forgive Elizabeth anything now and would never berate her ever again. She'd cared for her sister in such an exemplary way over the last ten years as her condition had worsened which couldn't have been easy.

She carried her tea back into the lounge and sighed. Maud didn't want to go back to being the big bad wolf and was enjoying the closeness they'd found. She smiled knowing Audrey would be cock-a-hoop if she could see them laughing and chatting together about old times.

Maud sat back in her chair and carefully placed her teacup and saucer onto the coffee table. She took a big gulp and furrowed her eyebrows in concentration.

She wrote, 'It was the day I collected Audrey from the coach station in Newcastle with the priest. It had been in the heat of the summer, and we'd stood around for forty minutes awaiting the late running coach from Carlisle.

When Audrey stepped off the coach, the priest had taken her small case and strode ahead.

I had put my arm around Audrey's shoulder and asked. 'You, okay?'

Audrey had turned to me, scowled, and said, 'What do you think? He was born on April Fool's Day – that's a sick joke- isn't it?'

She'd burst into tears, and I'd given her a handkerchief, taken her hand, and hurried her out of the station.

Maud scribbled all of this down and nodded in certainty. She was sure this was a genuine memory now and not a dream. Continuing to write slowly, she noticed how spidery her handwriting had become.

Audrey had been inconsolable for weeks. I had heard her crying into her pillow night after night. I'd tried a few times to get her to talk about the delivery and baby, but she'd pursed her lips, shaken her head sharply, and shuddered - obviously with the awful memories. And then the shutters had come down. Audrey had been an expert at shutting things out of her mind if she didn't want to think about them. Not another word was ever spoken about the adoption and her time in Carlisle.

Maud drained her tea now and sighed. She wasn't sure if it would do any good but at least she'd remembered something. They still had no name to use, however, they knew for definite it was a boy and his birthdate. Although Maud was lost off with modern day technology, she did

*know that on the tinternet thingy they could
trace people anywhere in the world. Maud knew
this because Sheila had told her many times.*

*She sneaked a ginger snap biscuit out of the
barrel on the table and remembered buying it
for Audrey in Tiverton when they'd come to visit
one year. Maud felt her eyes fill with tears at the
loss of her sister.*

Chapter Thirty Four

My stomach is rumbling, and I head down to the Entertainment Centre to order a pizza. While I wait for ten minutes, I wander past the few cars parked next to three big lodges with 'For Sale' signs. It's on the reception side of the path.

I stop at one car knowing it is not an English make and frown. I can drive but living in York city there's never a necessity. When I first got married, we had a car, but it had been hers not mine. I did pass my test but have driven very little since. And now, of course, Barbie has a car, and she loves to drive so if we go anywhere, she'll always say, 'I'll drive – it's my way of relaxing on the open road.'

Therefore, I couldn't say that I have a vast knowledge of cars like other men especially those who watch, Top Gear on TV with great enthusiasm. However, I do notice the driver's side is opposite to English cars and whip out my mobile. I Google the words, German cars, and discover the Volkswagen is one of their most popular makes.

I look at the licence plate and can see that it fits the criteria set out on Google. 'Standard German number plates use black print on a white background. There is a blue strip featuring the stars of the European Union and Germany's country code on the left. The registration number can have up to eight characters which are visually split into three clusters.'

I smile knowing the plate I'm looking at has exactly all of these details. This has to belong to Dennis. I wonder what the chances are that another German citizen would be staying here in Whitley Bay caravan park? Virtually none, I think and grin.

Dennis's appearance now clicks into place. The dark red chinos he wears and the collarless jacket which is typically Austrian. Along with the wavy, long moustache which reminds me of the Belgian detective, Hercule Poirot – definitely European I nod in satisfaction.

It seems too much of a coincidence that Dennis is from an area in Germany and Audrey had an affair with a German POW, but I figure that is jumping to conclusions.

I check my watch and wander back to collect my pizza. Heading back up to my caravan, I know the next question has to be - why has Dennis parked his car down here and not up at Ashley Mews like Jim and Kieran have done?

Dennis has his car tucked away out of sight, and nearer to the lodge which would have been handy if he'd had to drive Audrey down to the causeway on Monday night. I shake the thoughts from my mind as the smell of warm pizza floats up and my mouth waters. I put a spurt on and hurry up the road.

I look ahead and see Celia walking towards me with Rusty on his lead. Celia isn't just walking she seems to be almost skipping and is dressed in a bright, blue trouser suit. The dog starts yelping and straining on his lead as they near and I can see Rusty is pleased to greet me, or is it the pizza he can smell?

'Hello,' I say and with my free hand I bend to Rusty and tickle his ears. I peer behind her expecting to see Jim but there's no sign of him.

Celia notices and smiles. 'Jim is out with his friends playing golf. It's the first time he's been for weeks,' she says proudly.

I go along with her jubilant mood. 'Hey, that's great – he must be feeling better, is he?'

She doesn't just smile but grins now showing all her teeth. Gone is her usual tight-lipped version of a smile. 'Yes, and the best news ever is that Jim agreed and has been to see the doctor.'

'Well now, isn't that great, Celia,' I say feeling pleased for them both. 'I hope that it's good news.'

Celia nods. 'The doctor did a few simple memory tests which Jim got 100% right, but admitted to feeling in a low mood and worrying over trifling things,' she says. 'So, he's given Jim a course of anti-depressants and is arranging a scan with blood tests. The doctor said he'd had patients in the surgery following the pandemic suffering the same symptoms of worry and sadness.'

I think about this comment and decide it's understandable how people have reacted in different ways over the last few years we've been through. 'Yep, I suppose that's very true.'

She nods. 'So, whatever they find in the tests, we'll face it together head-on.'

'There's no other way, Celia,' I say. 'And Jim's a lucky man to have you by his side.'

Celia almost giggles and nonchalantly waves her hand. 'Now, Clive, be off with you - I won't keep you from your supper any longer.'

She tugs Rusty away and sets off jauntily down the road. I turn to look at her while fishing out the key from my pocket. She's like a new woman, I reckon. Celia has obviously been as worried about her husband as he has been about getting Alzheimer's. Which, of course, he may well still have.

I dive into my pizza straight from the carton and wolf it down while my mind works at a hundred miles an hour. How can I discover Dennis's back-history?

Folding up the empty pizza box, I figure an open confrontation is probably going to be the best and quickest way. And hey, if I make a fool of myself, well it won't be the first time.

I stand under the shower thinking of the questions to which we need answers. Why is he here from Germany? I suddenly remember him looking at the history of Whitley Bay in the library that day and frown. Did he have relatives that were here during the war? But most of all, we need to know where he was on Monday night?

Chapter Thirty Five

I wake early and decide to trail Dennis today. I can't rely upon bumping into him by chance - that might never happen. The more questions that come into my mind the more I want answers.

Taking a bowl of cereal, I head to the back of my caravan and sit on the short sofa where I've never sat before. I draw back the curtains and look out directly at the front of Dennis's caravan. His blinds are closed but it is early.

I munch into the cereal and remember last year how I'd followed someone for the first time. My work colleague had gotten involved in an on-line dating scam and the man she'd fallen for was suspicious to say the least. I had learned a few things that night of how to be inconspicuous amongst a crowd. How to be close enough to follow but not too close so they know I'm there.

Sitting in my boxer shorts, I decide to wear my black T-Shirt and jeans, so I won't stand out. However, I re-think this looking up at the brilliant sunshine outside. Black clothes only worked in winter on York's dark, eerie side-streets. Whereas here, if I'm dressed in dark colours, I'll probably be more noticeable because everyone is wearing white summery colours. I decide to wear my light chinos and beige T-shirt.

I shower and dress quickly then set up my laptop back on the sofa. I crane my neck around the side of Dennis's caravan and am well-placed to see him, when and if, he makes an appearance. I know I'll have enough time to grab my keys, lock up and set off behind him at a reasonable distance.

I look behind longingly at the veranda with my glorious sea view and sigh. This is more important if I want answers, which I do. I set my jaw in steely determination as Jason, my detective often does and smile.

Opening an email from Barbie my heart gives a little leap. She is definitely finishing her contract soon and ends her email with loads of small xxx. I think wistfully of kissing those lips of hers but shake myself back to concentrate on the front his caravan.

I'm rewarded for my vigilance within the hour when I see his blinds open a little. Not fully, but just enough to know he is up and doing something. I close down my document and prepare myself to leave feeling a shiver run up my back. It's the usual eerie one that makes me think something strange is going to happen.

And there he is, I think, jumping up from the sofa. I stare down the side of his caravan and see him lock his door and try the handle at least three times. Clutching my keys, I keep my eye on him then stop. Dennis has walked a few steps down his ramp but turns and returns to his door. Has he forgotten something? But no, he tries the handle once more, shakes his head and walks off again.

***

I'm out of my caravan like Jack Flash and cut over the grass to stay behind him. Although his tracksuit looks like it's seen better days, I can tell he's been used to a better standard of living and am desperate to know about his life and what he's doing here.

He strides down from Ash Mews towards reception and heads inside. I can't follow him into reception, so decide to hang around on the corner. There's an ice cream van parked up and I lick my lips – I can never resist. I'm not sure how long Dennis will be in reception and figure I've time to devour a cornet. I do so and lick at the soft ice cream which has a great flavour and is cooling me down.

Dennis reappears and turns the corner so quickly that he's right in front of me and I'm flustered. I wipe the cream from my lips with the back of my hand.

'That looks good,' he says. 'I've just been into reception to let them know I'm leaving tomorrow afternoon.'

I'm startled at this news. 'Oh, right,' I mutter. 'Are you going home?'

Dennis doesn't answer this question. I watch him chew at the bottom of his moustache and change the subject by saying, 'Hey, I'm reading your book - I got it from Amazon - it's a good story and I've stayed near that place in London.'

This floors me and even though I'm supposed to be questioning him I can't help but glow at the compliment. I stutter, 'O…oh that's great - thanks!'

I wonder how he knew my surname because I haven't told him and figure maybe Jim has. My brain kicks into gear and know if he's leaving tomorrow, I have to find out his connection to this caravan park and decide to go straight in with my main question.

The ice cream begins to drip on my hand, and I pull back my shoulders. 'Dennis, you know that I've been helping Liz,' I say. 'So, can I ask you where you were last Monday night when Audrey disappeared?'

I realise I've used a sharper tone to my voice mainly because I'm concerned about Audrey's death and not knowing about this man is bugging me. There's an awkward silence between us as a seagull squarks noisily up above on the reception roof.

Dennis draws his bushy eyebrows together in a severe frown. It's obvious he's not happy about being asked although I can't see his eyes because he's wearing mirrored sunglasses. I notice the rough red score marks on the back of his hands. A dermatological complaint, I wonder, Psoriasis?

He removes his sunglasses, stands with his legs planted wide and puts his clenched fists on his hips. His eyes are ablaze and seem to be protruding when he shouts, 'What the hell has it got to do with you - you're not the police!'

And he's right, I think startled at his raised
voice. He takes a step towards me and snarls,
'Just who the devil are you?'

I decide a change of mood is necessary if I'm
to get him to talk. I drop my shoulders and smile
trying to look more friendly sucking a big
mouthful of ice cream before it runs down the
side of the cornet. I'm just about to say, hey, I
didn't mean to upset you, when he moves
swiftly. With steady hands he grabs the hem on
the bottom of my T-shirt and pulls it up and
right over my head.

I'm plunged into darkness. My hand and the ice
cream cornet are trapped inside the T-shirt and
shoved up against my mouth. I gasp with shock.
My nose is full of ice cream, and I try to drag the
cornet away from my mouth. I'm spluttering
cream all over my face until with my free hand I
feel along the back of my neck and find the edge
of the T-shirt then pull it forwards and back over
my head.

Sun blinds my eyes and I gasp taking deep
breaths. I felt as though I was suffocating. I
relish the fresh air and try to wipe the wet, sticky
ice cream from my face using the back of my
hand. I chuck what is left of the cornet into the
waste bin behind the wall and frantically look
around for Dennis, but he's gone.

I spin around and see the back of his track suit
disappear behind the last caravan on the top row.
I know that even if I were to run after him, I
wouldn't catch up with his fast pace. I'm too

unfit. My young detective, Jason would give chase and arrest him. But, I'm not him. And, what would I accuse Dennis of doing? Is ramming an ice cream in someone's face classed as an assault?

The creamy dairy smell that previously was fresh and delicious is now making me feel sick. Droplets have dried and stuck to my fringe. I sneeze which sprays wet cream all over my face again. I pull the T-shirt off all together and with trembling legs and a bare chest, I slowly walk back to my caravan and the shower. My only hope is that I don't bump into Amber on the way. The sight of my bare chest may just tip her over the edge with excitement and I grunt all the way back.

***

The shower refreshes me, and I stand still letting the hot water soak down onto my face. Now that I've calmed down, I struggle to understand what has just happened. With a big sigh I decide my surveillance and sleuthing campaign was a total disaster, and amateur to say the least.

Really, I think drying my body, who did I think I was? And eating ice cream at such a moment was ridiculous. I seethe in annoyance with myself. Brushing my teeth, I gargle to rid my mouth of the cream flavour and recap over the whole encounter.

Dennis had taken me completely by surprise on all accounts. I hadn't been ready for any of his tactics which makes me frown. He'd rounded the corner quickly and had thrown me off kilter at first. Also, his praise over my book was another revelation and I had bumbled about in a stutter. The information that he is leaving tomorrow had sent me into panic mode because I want answers before he goes, and I'd used an accusatory tone in my question. This, I can see would have annoyed anyone.

However, by then I'd realised my mistake and was preparing to inject a more friendly vibe into the conversation. I had been ready for more verbal altercations, but not a physical attack on my body. I shake my head knowing I'd lost all self-control and had been badly rattled.

The thought makes me remember last year when I was mugged. How I had lain face down on the wet cobbles in a side street in the dark having been knocked to the ground. I'd been unable to move and had no control over my body while the mugger grabbed my money and ran off. I had been too shocked and terrified to move.

Was this the same as today? I make myself a hot cup of coffee and shrug. As Sherlock Holmes often says, it's the element of surprise that wins out every time. When a person is in a state of complete shock it's hard to react, which I reckon is what happened to me today. I simply hadn't been expecting the bodily assault.

I sip the coffee and munch a chocolate wafer bar. I start to see the humorous side to the incident especially with the ice cream and decide I might as well work with Ted Barker and his team of nincompoops. Grinning, I open my laptop.

Chapter Thirty Six

Dennis

'The bloody English!' Dennis yelled into his empty caravan. He crashed down onto the end of the bed feeling the soft mattrass sag beneath him. Who did they think they were ordering people about? Prying into everyone's business as if they had the right to know.

His heart still raced after running back up the road to Ashley Mews. His face burned hot, and he didn't know how to calm himself down. He ground his back teeth – it was at times like this that he wished he hadn't stopped smoking – he'd love a cigarette right now.

Dennis remembered his first few days here and how everyone he'd passed on the caravan park talked about the weather - had they no other topic of conversation? He grunted, English people were all snobs as far as he could see whether they were upper, middle, or working class.

He could never be certain if they were being sincere or sarcastic because every sentence they spoke started with the word, sorry. They prided themselves for having what they called, a stiff upper lip, but Dennis thought most of them were fools. Especially, the idiot, Clive with his ice cream. He clenched his fists. Well, he certainly wasn't going to get anything out of him that's for sure.

His heart began to slow, and he wrapped his arms around his body. He rocked and moaned with his chin to his chest thinking of Lena. It's how she always calmed him by holding him tight. When he'd first met Lena, it had been the one thing he loved about being close to her. And still was. The human contact. The loving gestures. The big hugs. She felt part of his own body.

It had been the first time in his life he'd experienced these loving acts. His mother, Greta loved him or so she told him often enough. But by the time he had reached five years old, she stopped hugging him. He remembered his father, Colin telling her off in his tyrannical way when he'd shouted, 'Stop mollycoddling the kid - he'll grow up like a pansy!'

Dennis hadn't know the significance of being a pansy, but later in life had sussed it out and had never forgotten the outburst that day. Therefore, as much as he'd tried over the years, he had never gotten along with his father. And now he knew the reason why - he wasn't a true Bavarian.

Although Colin had arrived in Garmish from Carlisle looking for Sebastian in his early twenties he had enough English characteristics that could never be offset by Greta and Sebastian. Dennis sighed and decided, even though Colin spoke fluent German he'd never quite grasped the pride associated with their culture like he had.

Thinking about Sebastian would calm him down, he thought and closed his eyes imagining him sitting by the fire. He remembered his grandfather telling him about the day Colin had stood outside his door. 'I'm your son,' he'd said. 'Can I come inside?'

And there Colin had remained until at the age of forty he married the younger Greta. Dennis knew from what Sebastian told him that aged nineteen he hadn't known Audrey was pregnant when he left Seaton Delaval Hall to travel home to Garmish. Sebastian had never married and said on many occasions, 'I wish I'd brought Audrey back here with me and married her.'

On the third day at the caravan park, Dennis had gone up to the hall and his gut churned thinking of Sebastian being a POW and labouring in the fields. He'd loved the history of the old Delaval family but interwoven in this had been the degradation of what his grandfather had gone through.

Dennis jumped up from the bed and pulled down his suitcase from the top of the wardrobe. He planned to take his leave. Clive wasn't the only one out to get him. Everyone seemed to want to punish and harass him - even the beautiful Amber who he'd thought had a hungry eye for him. As it turned out she gave other men the same look – even Clive, the joker.

The memory of Clive with the supercilious grin on his face and ice cream dripping down his hand made him seethe. The heat flushed through his body when he thought of Clive's brusque condescending tone almost accusing him of being with Audrey on Monday night.

Whether it be true or not, Dennis had wanted to knock him out, but instead remembered the T-shirt over the head manoeuvre that he had seen in a film at the cinema. And it had worked well. Clive wouldn't accuse him of assault because as a man it would make him look even more foolish than what he was. Which, Dennis decided was idiotic.

Now, he inhaled deeply trying to steady himself – he wanted to go on the rampage and smash the caravan to pieces. Dennis knew his OCD was spiralling out of control and struggled each day to hide the disorder. However, he still didn't think the medication would work and improve his state of mind. He'd stopped the tablets two months ago because they weren't making much difference although Lena thought they were. She'd often told him that he lost his grip on reality without the medication which he now thought was an absurd thing to say.

He was perfectly in the zone although had to admit that his social anxiety had worsened, and he felt trapped in the short term rather than taking a long distance view on his life. The inability to sleep and eat properly had re-surfaced, and he knew sometimes his walk was what Greta called, herky-jerky. Often his voice wobbled, and the profuse sweating was marking his clothes.

Opening drawers and cupboards he arranged his clothes on the bed ready to pack as temper still flowed through him. He stomped back and forth in the caravan picking up his belongings. He looked at his family tree chart and documents pinned on the wall which he'd done when he had first arrived and raged – how had this happened? Audrey was his grandmother, but she'd ignored him.

Last month, he'd gathered his courage and wrote two letters to her, but she'd not even had the decency to answer. He had rang the caravan park twice and left messages but was told Audrey wasn't available to take his call.

How dare they ignore him like this? He was part of their family and had been snubbed. When he thought of last Monday night Dennis had no regrets and knew once he got home to Bavaria and Lena, he would be fine again.

Chapter Thirty Seven

I'd wondered all night what to do about reporting Dennis to the police. Do I or don't I, had gone around in my head for most of the night. Along with dreams of suffocating in a dark black hole with a cover over my face that I couldn't remove. It hadn't been an easy T-shirt covering like in my real-life occurrence, but it was tight and fastened with heavy studs that try as I did, I couldn't open. I had woken twice sweating and clawing at my neck and knew this was going to be re-current nightmare which would be hard to shake off.

I head out onto my veranda. The sun isn't out, but I would rather be at the front of the caravan and as far away from Dennis as possible just in case he looked out of his blinds. I sigh. In a short space of twenty four hours, I'd gone from feeling upbeat and humorously calling him Slack-Jowls to feeling down-beat and intimidated by him. How had I let that happen?

I haven't told Barbie about the incident over the phone for two reasons. First, I know I'm going to sound foolish, which I suppose I was, and second, I know she'll worry about me while she's away. I've no problem telling Barbie when we get home because I'm more than used to owning up and feeling stupid with her. I try to bolster myself for the day ahead and think logically through the encounter with Dennis.

There are facts that I know for sure.

There has to be a link between him coming here from Germany, looking at the history of the area and Audrey's war-time soldier. There has to be – that's just too big of a coincidence.

He didn't answer my question about Monday night so I'm still none the wiser as to his whereabouts, although Jim did see his blinds open. This wouldn't be unusual for any other neighbour on the park, but in nine days of me staying in front of his caravan, open blinds were rare. If Dennis had been near the lodge on Monday night and did have something to do with Audrey's fall then he was strong enough to carry her without a problem, and he had a car to transport her down to the causeway.

I also know that he has a temper. I'd seen his eyes ablaze in anger and how with his fists clenched, he'd been ready to strike out – I just know it.

Thinking of Liz and Maud alone in the lodge, I shudder. If I add the timing issue, how he is planning to leave this afternoon, to all of the other details, I need to act now. I pick up my mobile, dial the number and ask for Inspector, Ted Barker.

I'm not relishing telling Ted about the assault and ice cream, but know it'll be necessary to convey the fact that Dennis may be violent, and how I'm concerned that the ladies are on their own.

A gruff voice answers with a simple, 'Yes?'

'It's Clive Thompson at the caravan park,' I say. 'I was with Liz when you came to see her?'

He grunts but doesn't speak. I take a deep breath and state the facts as I know them while he listens in silence.

Only once does he interrupt when I get to the encounter with Dennis and says, 'An ice cream, eh?'

I can almost see the amusement on his face and hear it in his words, but I push on. 'So, Inspector, I know he has a temper and is capable of violence,' I say. 'And the ladies are on their own in the lodge.'

I hear him sigh heavily then he answers. 'I'll send someone down.'

The line goes dead, and I know he's gone. I pull on my trainers and head down to the lodge.

***

Liz is hanging out washing on their line in the back garden when I arrive, and she waves me inside.

'Hey there,' she says. 'I was going to ring you later.'

I quip, 'You were?'

She grins. 'Yes, I rang St. Mary's in Carlisle yesterday and a nice lady told me that the person I need to speak with is back into the office on Wednesday and I'm to call back.'

I'd quite forgotten about the nursing home and smile. 'Well, that's good news – isn't it?'

She nods and takes a peg out of her mouth then pushes it into the waistband of a pair of trousers.

'And, I've wondered since Sunday about the man in the caravan behind you and why you wanted his address?'

I perch on the end of a sun lounger and smile. There're no flies on her, I think and know I should have rang last night. Liz needs to hear this now.

'Yes, well, I had an eventful day,' I say and slowly repeat everything I've just told Ted Barker.

She stops pegging out and hurries towards me dumping a jumper back into the laundry basket on the way. 'What?' She cries. 'And he's leaving this afternoon?'

I nod. 'Apparently, but maybe you could check with your computer if you register the details for departure?'

Liz flies inside the lodge and I hear her calling to Maud that she'll be back later. Pulling on a fleece jacket she grabs my arm and propels me out of the front garden. I hurry alongside trying to keep up with her while she gabbles.

'I knew there was something about him!' She shouts. 'And where is this bloody place, Bavaria? Somewhere in Spain? I've never trusted the bloody Spanish!'

Any other time, I'd hoot with laughter but know this isn't the time or place. I sigh instead realising Liz doesn't know that it's in Germany and hasn't put two and two together. She's breathing heavily now as we reach the reception doors and stops to catch her breath. Probably the cigarettes, I think but follow her inside as she swings open the door.

'Scoot!' She shouts at the young receptionist who gets up and scurries away from computer.

I smile reassuringly at the receptionist who hovers in the corner looking apprehensive.

Liz scrolls down the list of customers on the screen. I can tell she knows this spreadsheet like the back of her hand, after all, she probably set it up.

'Ahh, yes,' she says. 'He's checking out at four this afternoon but hasn't paid his bill yet.'

I point over her shoulder to his address on the screen then quietly whisper in her ear. 'Bavaria is in Germany, Liz.'

The colour drains from her face as she looks up at me. 'G...Germany?'

I nod. 'Now, I'm thinking it could be just a coincidence how he has arrived here, is interested in Whitley Bay history, and your mam had a fling with a German soldier, but maybe not?'

Liz jumps up and hurries through into the side room. She flings open a cupboard on the wall with row upon row of hanging keys then grabs a key ring in her hand. 'Well, we'll soon see about that!' She says hurrying back to me. 'Come, on, let's see what this weirdo is hiding in his caravan.'

She races back behind the desk then stops at the young receptionist and squeezes her arm. I can tell it's an apologetic gesture for snapping earlier and the squeeze tells her not to worry. I follow Liz out of the door.

Chapter Thirty Eight

We hurry along to Ash Mews but I'm keeping up with her this time. My stomach is churning not knowing what we'll find inside Dennis's caravan. I am not going to be brave and pretend I'm not scared, because after yesterday's encounter, I am.

I say, 'Look, Liz, maybe it's best to wait until the police get here before going inside.'

She stops and stares at me. 'Oh, no, I'm not waiting around for them. Going on past times they'll take ages to get here, if at all.'

'Well, I'm just thinking that he could be violent?'

Liz snorts, 'I'm not scared of him,' she says. 'Before we got the security officer on the park, I slept with a baseball bat under the bed.'

'Oh, wow,' I mutter.

'And, when Mam was younger, she was a force to be reckoned with,' Liz says furrowing her eyebrows. She pulls her fleece around her chest in a defiant manner. 'I've chucked more drunks out of the club than I care to remember.'

I can't help but smile and imagine the pair of them in their younger days. I know Dennis will probably be more scared of Liz than yours truly.

I nod, 'Okay, but is going inside not classed as trespassing, or something?'

Her face is still pale, but her eyes are wide and gleaming. She licks her red-painted lips. 'Trespassing,' she yells. 'I own the bloody caravan!'

I wince at her retort but can well understand the agitation. I take a deep breath and hold her arm. 'Right, if you insist but we'll only enter if he's not in there,' I say. 'If he is there let me try and talk to him first before barging inside – okay?'

Liz nods but I'm not convinced that she'll do as I've asked. I notice her hand is trembling when she puts the key in the lock and pulls down the handle.

Man-up, I think to myself and ease her aside. I take a tentative step inside the caravan and call out, 'Dennis!'

There's no answer and I can feel Liz's breath on the back of my neck. I try again taking another step inside. 'Dennis – are you there?'

Still no answer then Liz steps on the back of my trainer and pushes me aside in her hurry to get inside. She turns right, striding around the bedrooms and bathroom first then calls out, 'There's no sign of him here.'

I've walked into the lounge area and relaxed my shoulders. There's a suitcase and holdall standing in the corner obviously ready to go. I figure he must be out somewhere, but of course, we don't know for how long.

I turn around and gasp in shock at the wall opposite the TV. There's a whole display of records, certificates, newspaper cuttings, and right in the centre is the same photograph that Liz found under her mam's pillow.

I feel Liz behind me rather than see her and turn slowly. She gapes at the wall and slaps both her hands onto her cheeks. She gives a small squeal. 'OMG, who is he?'

I shake my head in wonder and trace a finger over the large box diagram with names on it and read. 'Well, it looks like the whole of his family tree is here on this huge display, and I think he's your nephew.'

She takes one hand from her face and grips my forearm. I can see her hand visibly shaking now when she says, 'Tell me how, Clive?'

'So, according to this, his father is Colin Muller (nee Miller) who was born and adopted in Carlisle.'

I trace my finger further up the boxes. 'And, his grandfather was Sebastian who was a POW at Seaton Delaval Hall.'

I turn to look at her with my finger over the old photograph. 'This soldier who your mam loved was Sebastian.'

Her face is ashen, and sweat is standing on her upper lip. I see her start to sway and ease her by the arm to the sofa unit. I can hear Barbie's voice in my ear saying, head between your knees if you're going to faint. I help Liz to do this and say, 'Take the deep breaths again, Liz.'

This poor woman has been through so much that my head spins with everything we've learnt. I can't help feeling justifiably proud of myself because I've known all along that there was a link and finally, we've found out about Dennis and, why he is here.

Liz is still breathing deeply then lifts up her head. 'Phew - that was a shocker,' she mutters.

I nod and squeeze her shoulder. 'Yeah, I knew there was a link between Dennis and this place, or he wouldn't be here, but really, Liz, I didn't see this coming.'

My ears prick at a noise outside. It's a man whistling, and my shoulders instantly rise in readiness. Maybe it's one of the gardeners – or is it, Dennis? I listen hard and at the same time pull Liz up onto her feet. It could have just been a holidaymaker passing the back of the caravan but I'm not willing to take the chance. I walk Liz towards the door so I can take a look outside.

We'd left the door ajar and the nearer I get, I hear footsteps of heavy boots. Dennis usually wears sandals so I'm thinking it can't be him, but this thought is instantly quashed as the door is flung wide open.

Liz and I both jump. Dennis is standing on the ramp outside the open door. There's a deafening silence between the three of us and I catch a glimpse of his car parked behind the ramp - we've obviously just caught him in time.

His shoulders pull back in the brown, collarless jacket as though his whole body is swelling up ready to challenge us.

'How dare you!' He bellows. The force of his voice makes me quiver a little, but I know the situation needs to be managed carefully in an effort to talk in a reasonable manner.

'Now, Dennis,' I begin but I'm not quick enough.

Liz yells, 'What do you mean – it's my bloody caravan!' She folds her arms across her chest. 'I've got every right to see what's inside here and what you've been up to?'

I put my hand out to him. Not in a handshake but with my palm uppermost as if in peace. 'Look, let's all sit down inside and talk this through.'

But Dennis ignores me and glares at Liz. 'You've ignored me since the day I arrived here,' he roars. 'And now that I'm leaving you are both in here snooping around at my stuff.'

Liz takes a step forward towards him. It's a confident step and I can see she means business – she's obviously not afraid of him. Her face is bright red, and her eyes are huge. 'What do you mean, ignored you?' She shouts. 'We've only just found out who you are!'

I watch Dennis's shoulders slacken and he backs away from her. I was right before when I thought that he'd be more frightened of Liz than me, but know I still need to protect her if necessary. I step up behind as she strides further towards Dennis and is now outside on the ramp. She places her hand on the white railing and I see her knuckles are white as she grips hard.

'Why didn't you just say who you were the day you came?' She yells. 'I haven't got a bloody crystal ball – we didn't know you even existed!'

Although she still has her voice raised, I can tell there's not as much anger and temper left in her. 'I only found the photograph of the soldier when Mam died last week.'

Dennis is well and truly deflated now and has backed himself further away from Liz and down towards the bottom of the ramp. I watch him chew at the bottom of his wavy moustache.

I'm not sure if it's the mention of Audrey mixed with Liz's aggression that has caused the change, but I relax a little hoping the threat of violence has passed. I don't comment knowing this conversation has to be between them but stay right behind Liz just in case.

'She laughed at me,' Dennis says. 'She was my grandmother and snubbed me when I saw her in the garden.'

And I know. In that split second with his three words, in the garden, I know it was Dennis who killed Audrey. Be it accidental, or not, he had done it.

I watch Liz raise her eyebrow. 'You saw her last Monday night?'

Dennis nods slowly and begins to scratch at the back of his hands. 'It made my b…blood boil,' he stuttered. 'She gave my father away without a moment's thought and stood there grinning like she didn't care what I was suffering.'

Liz is in front of him now and shouts, 'But she had dementia! Mam laughed and grinned at everybody some days when she didn't know who she was – let alone anyone else!'

Dennis crumbles now. 'W…what?'

'It's called Alzheimer's Disease,' Liz says. 'And she was ninety years old, for God's sake!'

I'm not sure if he recognises the name, Alzheimer's, but I reckon they must have the same disorder in Germany. His face is flushed now as he stares at Liz.

I see him suck in his cheeks which make his Slack-Jowls wobble. 'I…I came down to your lodge at night and saw you go inside. I was going to talk to you, but I lost my confidence,' he murmurs wringing his hands. 'You see, I haven't been well. I'm not sleeping or eating properly, and my head is all over the place!'

Liz simply nods but doesn't take her eyes from his face.

Dennis blinks a few times and catches a hitch in his throat as he continues, 'So, I peered through the window at my grandma, and she waved. The next thing she was outside, and I stupidly thought she had recognised me.'

'It's the eyes,' Liz says flatly. 'Mam had gone on about big, brown eyes, and you have the same as your grandfather – the soldier in the photograph.'

Finally, I think, Liz has put the puzzle together on her own. I can tell she's more capable of rational thought now she knows the full story.

I watch Dennis's eyes which look like they're rolling and he's obviously distraught. He begins to cry with big sobs that seem to rack his solid chest.

'S…she tripped on the grass and fell backwards then hit her head. I saw the pool of blood coming from the back of her head and a trickle of blood from her ear,' he croaks in between sobs. 'I picked her up in my arms - she was light like a doll. But I was terrified because I knew she was d…dead,' he gabbles now. 'I…I was going to carry her inside to you but knew how bad it would look, so I laid her flat on the steps of the causeway and ran off.'

Chapter Thirty Nine

We are at the bottom of the ramp now at the small white gate and I'm not sure how this is going to end. I'm considering ringing a doctor for Dennis when I hear a siren in the background. The police are obviously coming through the main gates into the caravan park.

I can tell by the way Dennis jumps back into an alert state that he's heard it too. In a flash, Dennis pulls out a pistol from the inside of his pocket and grabs Liz from behind with his arm around her neck. She screams and I rush towards them. Dennis is aiming the pistol on her forehead as I stand in front of them both.

'Stay back!' Dennis shouts, 'Or I'll shoot her!'

My heart is pounding, and I shout, 'No, Dennis, this isn't the way to do things!'

A police car screeches up to a halt on the grass. I see the young blonde policewoman jump out of the front and Ted climb out of the back.

Dennis's eyes are wild. Sweat is pouring down his forehead and he starts to stamp his feet. He yells again, 'All of you - get away from me!'

I stand still terrified to move any closer to Liz in case he does what he's threatening. I see Ted whisper to the policewoman then step closer to us.

'Now just calm down,' Ted says with his arms held up high as if in defence.

I literally feel like striking Ted because of his ineptitude. I hear the policewoman calling on her radio for the armed response unit.

My mind races. Dennis will have heard the call as I have, so he must know this isn't going to end well. This might just tip him over the edge.

Silence descends upon us all as if we are in a tableau in the theatre up at Seaton Delaval Hall. But this isn't make-believe, I rage, it's happening for real and I'm desperate to help Liz. Not taking my eyes from her, I see Amber and the gigglers out of the corner of my eye. It's obvious everyone has come out to see what's happening.

I hear Celia scream and then shout, 'OMG, he's got a gun!'

The atmosphere hangs heavy. All I can hear are the noisy seagulls above Dennis's caravan running along the roof. Suddenly, I think of Maud, and know she needs to be here.

If Celia is there, then Jim won't be far behind. I call out loudly, 'Jim, will you fetch Aunt Maud?' He doesn't reply but I hear Rusty barking as if in response.

Everyone is deciding what to do next, especially me. I know from experience the police will make the situation worse. Keep him talking, I think, and try to distract Dennis.

Liz is like a statue. She is white faced and whimpering. Gone is her bolshy attitude and loud voice. I can see she's terrified. But who wouldn't be with a gun at your forehead?

I think back to the details from Seaton Delaval Hall and begin to describe what it must have been like during the war for Sebastian and

Audrey. I'm talking quietly to Dennis and focus all my attention upon his face which is almost purple now. He stops stamping so I hope I'm having some type of effect upon him.

'Your grandfather, Sebastian must have been a great guy to get through what he did as a POW?'

I see Dennis's shoulders slacken a little and know I've got him engaged. He doesn't answer but grunts.

'And,' I say. 'I'm wondering if your Aunt Liz has any more of Audrey's old photos?'

Liz's eyes blink rapidly looking around and I know she is listening. I take another step towards Dennis then feel Ted at my left side. His big shoulder is against mine covering some of my chest. My opinion of him increases rapidly. In his bullet-proof vest, I can tell he is ready to step in if the worst happens, although he doesn't issue a warning.

Ted doesn't need to because sweat is running down my back and my mouth dries up as I'm talking. My heart is banging with blood pumping in my ears, and I know any minute now, Dennis could pull the trigger and we'll be goners.

Dennis shrugs his big shoulders and stares directly at me - he clears his throat then mutters, 'Maybe.'

'And it's not fair to punish Liz and Audrey for something they knew nothing about or at least your aunt didn't - did you Liz?'

Liz tries to squirm a little then looks up at Dennis. 'No, I didn't. Mam was so demented that she didn't know who anyone was,' she whispers. 'Although, she used to call the ice cream man, Colin even though his name is Dave. So, maybe in her confused state she was still thinking of your father being her baby?'

This is the moment, I see Dennis slacken his grip around her throat. He stares down at her face and asks, 'Really?'

Suddenly, two things happen at once. I see Liz spin around in his arms and I rush towards them. She promptly lifts her leg and knees him in the groin. I reach them and grab Dennis's arm as his knees buckle in pain. I hold his arm up high and feel Ted and the policewoman right behind me. Dennis drops the gun to the ground and falls to his knees in front of us all.

'You, bastard,' Liz shouts then kicks him again on his backside.

The policewoman grabs Liz holding her back and she crumbles in her arms. Tears are streaming down her face, and she is visibly shaking from head to foot. I take some deep breaths in and out slowly just as I've taught Liz to do and smile as two other police officers drag Dennis up then cart him away.

I hear Ted reading the police caution. 'You do not have to say anything, but it may harm your defence if you do not mention when questioned something which you later rely on in court. Anything you do say may be given in evidence.'

The police woman lets go of Liz and she flies into my arms crying. I hug her tight and rub her back. 'It's over,' I say. 'You're safe now.'

I feel an old fragile hand on my elbow and turn to see Maud. Liz leaves me and heads into her aunt's arms. 'Young man, I can't thank you enough for rescuing Elizabeth,' she says. 'I'll always be eternally grateful.'

I smile at them both. My cheeks flush as usual at the compliment. 'Aww, it's okay, I...I just did my best in a scary situation.'

Maud smiles. 'I'll take Elizabeth home now – but would you come for a stiff shot of brandy?'

I decline knowing Liz is still in shock and needs some time to herself. But I can't help thinking about the future. What will Liz do about Colin? Will she want to contact him?

I hurry back along the ramp inside the caravan. I remember seeing some of Dennis's business cards lying on the bench. Quickly, without touching them, I take a photo with my mobile and hear Ted shout, 'Hey, get out of there – it's a crime scene!'

Back outside, I read his contact details with a landline telephone number. Bingo, I think and grin.

Chapter Forty

Rusty runs up to me and I kneel down sinking my face into his soft neck for comfort. I could do with a cuddle from someone and wish Barbie was here. Although, I wouldn't admit to it, but my brush with danger has left me a little wobbly.

Celia asks, 'Are you okay?'

I give a half-hearted smile. 'I think so,' I say. 'But I've never faced a man with a gun before.'

She nods. 'Okay,' she says taking charge of the situation. 'You'll come to ours for a while and I'll get you a strong cup of tea.'

Jim takes my hand and shakes it as we slowly walk around Dennis's caravan and back to our doors. I look longingly at my veranda hoping for some peace and quiet but follow Celia inside their caravan. Rusty immediately jumps up on my knee as I sit down onto the sofa unit. My legs stop trembling as I stroke and fuss Rusty.

Celia hurries into the kitchen area and begins to open and close cupboards. I can tell she's going to feed me and sigh with relief. My stomach is growling, and my throat has almost dried up - I'm gasping for a drink. She rustles up beef sandwiches and Battenburg cake.

I wolf it down talking rapidly with Jim who wants to know all about what happened. I explain about his family tree and his father, Colin and grandfather, Sebastian.

'I felt a bit sorry for him at first because he's obviously suffering from poor mental health.

But this soon disappeared when he confessed to what he'd done with Audrey,' I say. 'And I know his mind is warped and twisted, but all the same, the amount of grief his actions caused were totally unnecessary. Of course, it had been an accident when Audrey fell, but if only he'd alerted Liz, then maybe something could have been done to save her instead of carting her down to the causeway.'

I look at Jim in his cream slacks and brown shirt. Gone is the ravaged look on his face that he's seemed to wear over the last few days. I know like Celia, he is probably relieved after his visit to the doctor. I remember how I'd originally thought that he could have had something to do with Audrey's disappearance and subsequent death. My cheeks flush. He's just an ordinary man having a few problems and I curse my dubious thoughts.

'Thanks for bringing Maud over to the scene,' I say. 'I knew she'd want to be there and was conscious that she didn't know anything about it all.'

He nods and we talk about the police and what will happen to Dennis.

Jim raises an eyebrow. 'Not that I'm an expert on guns, but to me it looked like an old one from the war – maybe it belonged to Sebastian?'

'Could be, I suppose, but all I know is that it was terrifying looking at it on Liz's forehead.'

As I leave the caravan, Celia says, 'We've been so glad to have you as a neighbour, Clive, you've been fantastic throughout this sorry state of affairs.'

I wave my hand nonchalantly and return to my veranda with just me and my laptop. It's not easy to settle and I fight against ringing Liz or going over to see her. However, I remember the business card and text her a message with the photograph.

'Hope you've managed to settle down after the shocking revelations with Dennis and the standoff? Here is his home address and phone number. I reckon it'll be a lead into contacting Colin, if and when you're ready.' I end the message with a smiley face emoji.

She answers straight back with a big thank you and says she's doing okay.

Around five o'clock, Barbie is on Zoom. I go through the whole incident all over again.

'You look exhausted,' she says. 'Get a good night's sleep and I'll see you soon.'

Climbing into my bed later I think of her last sentence and sigh knowing I've another three days before she's in my arms again. I hug the pillow wishing it was her.

***

Next morning, the police ring and ask me to go to the lodge so Liz and I can both make our statements. I shower and dress in my chinos and blue T-shirt. Smiling to myself, I figure it's not a good idea to wear an old vest and shorts when I'm with Maud.

I wonder why being in the presence of an old lady fills people with respect - it had done with Liz in her Sunday dress for church. It's tradition and family values, I reckon sauntering down Ash Mews. I do this with Barbie's Mam when I visit and wonder, if my own grandma had lived would I have been the same with her? Although she had no airs and graces, I know I would still have respected her.

When I arrive, the young policewoman is in the garden sitting with Liz. They both have their heads bent over a clipboard and I figure she is doing her statement.

Liz looks up and calls, 'Morning, Clive, go-on inside and Aunt Maud will make you a cuppa.'

I nod and head inside calling, 'Hello…'

Maud hurries out into the hall. 'Ah, Clive, how lovely to see you,' she says. 'Now, have you had breakfast?'

I have had a bowl of cereal but tell a white lie because I can smell bacon wafting in the kitchen. 'Er, no, I haven't actually.'

She heads into the kitchen muttering, 'Young people don't know how to start the day properly.'

I sit down on the sofa and look around remembering my first few visits here when Liz was in a state of shock, and then meeting Maud, and the floundering Ted Barker. It seems a long time ago now.

Liz breezes in looking better than she has done for days wearing pink jazzy trousers. She says,

'It's your turn now. It didn't take long, and you should be much quicker being a writer yourself.'

'Ah, I don't know about that,' I chuckle.

Liz smiles. 'Oh, and I rang Dennis's house this morning and spoke to his fiancé, Lena. She was pleasant although obviously in shock about what he's done but has given my number to Colin, therefore, it'll be up to him if he wants to have contact with me.'

I nod. 'Hey, that's great, so the ball is in his court now.'

Liz seems to have bounced back very quickly, maybe too quickly. Perhaps she'll suffer later from delayed shock. I know this is the way of our brains protecting us initially to block out traumatic events, like post-traumatic stress disorder, which is a psychological shock where symptoms arise days after an incident.

'But how are you really?' I ask. 'I hadn't thought I would sleep much last night, but I did. – maybe the nightmares will come later?'

She nods. 'Well, I keep feeling a bit panicky but distract myself and try to push the image of the gun out of my mind,' she says rubbing her forehead. 'The gun felt cold which I would never have expected – would you?'

'Nope,' I say shaking my head. Fleetingly, the memory of facing Dennis with the gun comes into my mind and a shiver runs up my back.

'And you were amazing keeping him talking,' she says smiling. 'With every word you said I could feel his grip slackening.'

I can tell she wants to keep the recap light-hearted so, I joke. 'Well, that knee in the groin tactic was pretty darn impressive.'

She gives a throaty laugh. 'Oh, I've used it once or twice over the years,' she says patting the back of her hair.

I laugh out loud knowing she's making light of the situation, but if that's the way she's coping, then that's fine.

I start to walk along the hall when Liz squeezes my arm. 'And thanks again for everything – you saved my life which is something I'll never forget,' she says. 'You will always be my hero.'

'And mine, too,' says Maud popping her head out of the kitchen door.

I head outside with burning hot cheeks and join the policewoman. Liz is right – it doesn't take long to do the statement. I set out the facts from the beginning of the incident in Dennis's caravan to the police dragging him away. I thank the policewoman for their help and assistance yesterday and she waves goodbye.

Back inside the lodge, I sit down with Liz on the sofa and Maud hands me a bacon and sausage bap with heaps of brown sauce – it's delicious and I swoon over her with thanks.

'So,' Liz says, 'Apparently, the coroner is going to release the body soon for our funeral.' I smile in between mouthfuls of the bap. 'Hey, that's great - you'll be able to put all your plans into action then and say goodbye properly.'

The landline rings which startles me and Liz reaches over to answer. She holds her hand over the mouthpiece and whispers, 'It's Colin!'

I grin and listen to Liz's side of the conversation. Maud looks excited too, and fiddles with her pearls.

I watch Liz's animated face as she answers him. 'Yes, I was gobsmacked as well to hear about you. I didn't know you existed until I found an old photo hidden in Mam's room. Of course, now I know the soldier was called Sebastian.'

I see Liz's smile fade which is probably with a flashback to yesterday. 'I know,' she says. 'We didn't even know who Dennis was until yesterday when we found all the family tree papers and certificates in the caravan. If we'd known I'm sure I could have sorted something out with him.'

I try to imagine his side of the conversation when she answers.

'Well, at first he did seem to be very anxious and when he told us about what he'd done with Mam, he just seemed to flip,' she says. 'And I'm sure you're right that he's not usually a bad person.'

Liz looks at us and raises an eyebrow as if to say, yeah right.

I can see her concentrating and then she grins. 'Oh, right, tomorrow? Well, that'll be just great, and I'd love to meet you, too,' she says. 'In fact,

Mam's sister, my Aunt Maud is here so you can meet her too.'

Maud looks at me and nods in obvious pleasure.

'Okay, so take care on the flight with your walking stick and I'm sure Dennis will be glad to see you – he'll have had time to calm down now in a cell overnight.'

Liz takes a gulp of her tea then continues, 'A hotel? No, way, you're not staying in a hotel – you can stay here in one of our lodges,' she says pulling back her shoulders. 'You're family, so neither me, nor Aunt Maud, would hear of that.'

She replaces the receiver and grins. 'So, you'll have heard all of that - apparently, Colin has bad arthritis now, but knows Dennis will need him, so he's booked a flight to come over tomorrow morning from Munich. He sounds really nice – nothing like his obsessional weird son,' she says. 'Although Colin reckons, he didn't know Dennis had become so consumed with the family history.'

Liz grabs her mobile, presses a button, and says, 'I want Blyth Lodge which is empty cleaned now to within an inch of its life,' she says. 'And I'll be over in an hour to inspect it – I've got a very important guest coming to stay.'

I grin, squeeze her shoulder, and head out of the door. I can see Liz is in full manager mode now and know she's going to be fine.

Chapter Forty One

I'm sitting in the lodge the next afternoon with Liz, Maud, and Colin. He arrived an hour ago and all the introductions were made. The lounge is gleaming, and Maud is wearing what looks like her Sunday best outfit of a bright-blue suit and frilly white blouse. Even Liz has donned slim black trousers and a red blouse.

The atmosphere at first had been a little tense, but at the same time entertaining especially over tea, sandwiches, and cake. We've talked about the weather, his flight, and he has explained about his arthritis.

Colin is sitting now with a framed photograph in his hand of Audrey. 'I'm so pleased to see a photograph of Mam at last. I'd longed for this growing up because I had no idea at all of who she was?'

Maud is sheepish, but I can tell she is delighted to meet him. 'Well, as I've explained to Elizabeth and Clive – it was a different life back in the 1940s and your mam didn't really have a choice – we women never did.'

Colin shakes his head. 'I can't imagine what she and you must have gone through, and I can't tell you how thrilled I am to know I've a half-sister and a great aunt,' he says and then frowns. 'But at the same time, I'm so dreadfully sorry about what Dennis did with her in the garden and to you both, yesterday. I can't understand what's gotten into him – he must have had a complete breakdown.'

We all nod together and Liz sighs. 'He did look completely off his head.'

I keep staring from Colin to Liz noting the likeness which of course is from Audrey. I say, 'I can't stop looking at you both – although you have different eyes - the similarity in your features is remarkable.'

Liz smiles, 'I know, I can see myself in you too, Colin?'

Colin grins. Big, brown eyes twinkle in his wrinkly face. 'Same here, which is what I never felt with my adoptive parents in Carlisle,' he says. 'They had two girls, and I knew growing up that I was different and never felt part of the family. I left at twenty and traced Sebastian through the army and the help of a nurse at St. Mary's home who had been particularly close to Audrey. She'd known all about Sebastian from Audrey's story and the ski resort where he was from. All I knew was that I was born on April Fool's Day and set off to find him.'

I'm transfixed by his account and ask him to continue.

'Well, I turned up outside Sebastian's front door, told him I thought I was his son, and he took me in,' he says. 'I never left his side again because for once I felt at home. My father often said that he wished he had brought Audrey back with him and married her because she'd been the love of his life.'

Maud gasps loudly. 'Oh, dear,' she sniffs and pulls out her lace handkerchief. 'If only we'd known – everything was upside down when the war ended and, of course that's when Audrey discovered she was expecting you.'

I see her eyes fill with tears and shake my head at the sadness of it all. I wonder what part Colin might play in Liz's life now that Dennis has tried to harm her. And even though Liz knows Dennis was suffering from poor mental health will she want to try? I hope she does because after all, Colin is her family and I think she'll regret it if she doesn't.

Colin says, 'I'll contact the police in the morning and try to see Dennis, if possible,' he says. 'Then I'll be able to understand exactly what he has being charged with and if he needs medical treatment.'

Liz gets up out of the chair. 'Shall I walk you over to the lodge I've got ready for you to stay in - then you can unpack and settle-in while Aunt Maud prepares an evening meal for us.'

I make my excuses and leave them all wandering back towards my caravan.

***

A little way up the path, I hear a toot and swing around to see Barbie step out of a taxi. She pays the driver while I'm flying down to greet her and scoop her up into my arms. I feel close to tears while she giggles and wraps her arms around my neck. 'Surprise, surprise,' she whispers, and I throw my head back and laugh.

We spend two glorious days down on Whitley Bay beach and fortunately Barbie loves the painting of St. Mary's Lighthouse in the Art Links Café, so we buy it to take home. The next morning, I pack up and reluctantly leave the veranda and sea view. I know the painting will always remind me of this caravan park holiday.

We are getting into a taxi which will take us to the metro station and then into Newcastle for the train home. Barbie is sitting in the back of the taxi while I lift the suitcases into the boot.

I hear Rusty bark and he rushes up for one last pet and fuss. I look up to see Celia and Jim wave from their caravan door. Amber and the gigglers call goodbye from their veranda and as the taxi passes reception, Liz, Maud and Colin are waving to us.

I lean in towards Barbie and stroke her hair. 'Ah, it'll be nice to get home to York where it's peaceful and quiet rather than all the shenanigans in this caravan park.' I say and sigh. 'So much for a restful holiday, eh?'

Barbie teases.' Oh, stop, you've loved every minute of it all!'